THE BALL CAME TO HER SO HARD it
stung her fingers, but Andrea clenched her teeth,
dribbled across the lane, and shot a sweeping
hook shot which bounced around the rim and fell
in.

She clapped her stinging hands to show Jill
nothing was wrong, and then took her own place
in the passing line as her teammates clapped and
cheered.

"All right, Andrea!" Paula called. "Way to hit
the sky hook."

Sky hook, Andrea thought. That's what she
needed right now. A hook to come down out of
the sky and pull Jill up and give her a good
shaking. *Okay, God, reach down and do something to
Jill.* If only it could be that easy. . . .

For adventure, excitement, and even romance . . .
Read these Quick Fox books:

Dawn's Diamond Defense by Dan Jorgensen

Crystal Books by Stephen and Janet Bly
1 Crystal's Perilous Ride
2 Crystal's Solid Gold Discovery
3 Crystal's Rodeo Debut
4 Crystal's Mill Town Mystery
5 Crystal's Blizzard Trek
6 Crystal's Grand Entry

Marcia Books by Norma Jean Lutz
1 Good-bye, Beedee
2 Once Over Lightly
3 Oklahoma Summer

ANDREA'S BEST SHOT

DAN JORGENSEN

Chariot Books
David C. Cook Publishing Co.

For Susan, Kari, and Becky, and all the girls
on all of my teams

A Quick Fox Book

Chariot Books is an imprint of David C. Cook
Publishing Co.
David C. Cook Publishing Co., Elgin, Illinois 60120
David C. Cook Publishing Co., Weston, Ontario

ANDREA'S BEST SHOT
© 1985 by Dan Jorgensen
Cover design by Graphcom Corporation
Cover illustration by Jim Cummins
First printing, 1985
Second printing, 1988
Printed in the United States of America
92 91 90 89 88   6 5 4 3 2

Library of Congress Cataloging-in-Publication Data

Jorgensen, Dan.
    Andrea's best shot.
    (A Quick fox book)
    Previously published as: Sky hook.
    Summary: The new coach rekindles Andrea's interest in
joining the junior high basketball team, but she's not so sure
about being friendly with one of the other players.
    [1. Basketball—Fiction. 2. Schools—Fiction]
I Title.
PZ7.J7688An 1988   [Fic]   87-33760
ISBN 1-55513-860-8

Contents

1
The Doormats

"Hey, Andrea! Wait up!"

Andrea paused near the classroom door at the sound of Matt's voice and smiled as he hurried over.

"Hi," he said, nearly bumping into her in his rush. "You look nice today." He grinned. "Just thought I'd tell you."

Andrea grinned back, and all the freckles across her nose seemed to dance. She was tall and big boned for a 13-year-old, but with the natural grace of an athlete.

"Thanks," she said, brushing her sandy-colored hair back over one ear. She glanced at Matt as they started out of the classroom. He was a really nice, cute, athletic guy. "Just a couple more days till school starts," she said, as they walked out the door. "You nervous?"

"A little. Kinda nice being the oldest ones, though."

Andrea nodded. It would be their last year at Brown Junior High. Eighth grade. "I'm nervous *and* excited. Jill thinks I'm crazy because in *her* opinion school's such a drag. But there's always so much to do. Band, chorus, sports—"

"Jill likes the sports," Matt said dryly. "Everybody knows that."

Jill was in the eighth grade, too, and had spent the last half hour of Sunday school flirting with Matt. Andrea couldn't tell if he liked it or was embarrassed by it. At that very moment, they heard Jill calling their names.

Matt grimaced slightly as Jill came hurrying down the hall and slid in on his other side.

"Hey, Matt, you planning on playing football?" she asked, with hardly a glance at Andrea.

He nodded.

"Oh, great. You'll be super, I just know it!" She said it with a sort of syrupy sound in her voice, and this time it was Andrea's turn to make a face. Up until the past summer, Jill had been a rough-and-tumble tomboy who looked upon boys as athletic buddies. Now, all of a sudden, she was trying to be some great lover or some dumb thing like that.

"I'm going out for basketball again," Jill announced. "Maybe we'll have a better team this year, but I doubt it. Especially since the twins moved away. They were our best players, and we didn't have that great a team before."

That's for sure, Andrea thought. The Scoopers had been 2-12 last year, and the games they had won were close.

Andrea had been out for cross-country and was planning to run again. She'd rather be playing basketball, but the program was so poor there was very little chance for success. And, in cross-country, she'd have the chance to make the Sturgis High team if she worked hard enough at it.

With the state athletic system set up the way it was, eighth graders could compete on high school teams. She had to choose between the two sports because girls' basketball was in the fall and coincided with cross-country.

Still, she really thought a lot about basketball, especially since she and Jill shot baskets together. Right now, though, she wished Jill would disappear into the woodwork and leave basketball out of the conversation.

Surprisingly, Matt turned Jill's chatter into another chance to talk to Andrea.

"You going out for the basketball team this year?" he asked Andrea. "You should, you know. You're pretty good."

The trio stopped as their new Sunday school teacher, Mr. Forrest, walked up behind them. They parted to let him pass, but he stopped instead and joined in the conversation.

"Did I hear you three talking basketball? I'm pretty interested in that myself. I used to play a lot—back in high school. That was before my accident. Couldn't play as much once I got this." He gestured toward his stiff left leg. "Had a really bad break, and I've had this bad limb ever since. But I still love the game."

"I was just telling Andrea she should go out," Matt said. "She's good, and they could really use her size."

"I agree," Jill chipped in. "I'm maybe the biggest player we've got right now!"

The others looked at her in surprise, then they burst into laughter with her. Jill was tomboyish and tough, but size was not one of her attributes. She was barely five foot four.

"Well, I'm sorry to hear that," Forrest said. "I know the new coach quite well, and he was hoping to have some players with height."

"Naw, we don't have any height or much else, either," Jill said. "We might've been okay this year, but our two best players moved away. It'll be a long year." She put a lot of emphasis on the word *long* and grinned. "But we have fun."

"That's good," Forrest said. "Matt's right, though, Andrea. If you have an interest in basketball, you'd probably add a lot to the team."

"Oh, I don't know," Andrea began. "I think I'll be trying out for the cross-country team. I did some running last year, and I think they'll let me on the high school team this year if I keep improving. I really like basketball, but I'm not as good as these two let on."

"She is, too," they said together.

"She just doesn't like playing on a losing team," Jill added. "But we like her anyway."

"Yeah," Matt agreed. "She's kind of cute, you know." He gave her a quick sideways glance, and Andrea blushed up to the roots of her sandy-colored hair. Jill stared at both of them in surprise, started to say something, then clammed up.

"Well, I have to take off," Forrest said. "Enjoyed our Sunday school class today. See you all next week." He walked away and joined his wife and two little girls, who were waiting by the church entrance.

"I think Mr. Forrest is going to make Sunday school pretty interesting," said Matt. "Maybe even fun."

Tom Forrest was a new member of their congregation. He and his family had moved to Sturgis from Colorado just a few months before. His outgoing personality and enthusiastic teaching were a welcome change from last year's classes, and Andrea felt hopeful that now Jill's attendance would be regular. She was always encouraged when Jill did good things—like coming to Sunday school.

"Class definitely seems better than last year," Andrea agreed. "I think it's going to be a great year!"

"Well, I've gotta go," Matt said. "See you in school."

The girls watched him go; then Jill turned to Andrea.

"Well. 'She's kind of cute, you know,' " she mimicked. "I wouldn't have made a move on him if I had known you two were in love!"

"Oh, come off it!" Andrea said. "He's just a friend. I've got lots of boys for friends."

"That was more than just a *friend* look he was giving you." Jill gave Andrea a little push on the shoulder, and then skipped neatly aside as Andrea swung a handful of papers at her. Laughing, the pair went outside to find Andrea's mom and their ride home.

Later that afternoon, as Andrea bounced her basketball in the driveway and took jump shots at the hoop on the garage, she thought about Forrest's and Matt's urging her to join the girls' team. She put up a fifteen footer and watched it skip off the back of the rim and into the bushes alongside the drive. The program was so down and out, and some of the girls on the team were so negative. Besides that, she hadn't liked last year's coach, and she didn't know a thing about whoever the new coach would be. Although, if he was a friend of Mr. Forrest's, maybe he wouldn't be too bad.

She grabbed the ball and said aloud, "Andrea Atchinson takes the ball outside! Two seconds left! She shoots!" She fired off a twenty footer from deep in the bushes and let out a little shout and punched her fist in the air as the ball passed neatly through the hoop and rippled the net.

An appreciative whistle made her start in surprise, and she looked up to see Forrest, clad in a jogging outfit, panting at the end of the drive.

"Sorry. I didn't mean to startle you," he apologized. "But that was pretty fair shooting."

She retrieved the ball and grinned. "Sure, now if they would only grow some bushes on the court. I can shoot great from the bushes!"

They laughed together, and he walked over to join her.

"I was out jogging and saw you shooting. Say, you're a runner—want to jog along for a ways? I'm going out to the V.A. and back. That's about a mile from here, isn't it?"

"Sure," she nodded. "Guess I could use a couple of miles today. I've been doing a lot of running, but probably not enough yet if I really want to make the team. Let me put my ball in the garage and I'll join you."

She rolled the ball inside and trotted down to join him. They started along the main highway toward the V.A. Hospital, which was down the road and directly across from the high school. In a few days, she'd probably be running this route regularly during the five- and ten-mile "warm-up" runs for cross-country.

They ran in silence until they neared the hospital. Forrest limped to a walk. "Got to take it a little easy," he explained. "I try to run about a mile, then walk a quarter or so. Leg hurts a lot sometimes, but I hate sitting around doing nothing."

Andrea smiled appreciatively and nodded.

"Me, too. That's why I like to shoot baskets once in a while. I like running, but sometimes it gets a little boring."

They walked in silence for about a hundred yards before Forrest spoke.

"You know, I was serious about that basketball thing this morning. I always got a lot out of the game myself, and I think it's one of the best sports in high school. Now, when you're in junior high, it's a good time to sharpen your skills. With your size and obvious ability—"

"I got lucky on that shot you saw," she interrupted.

"Well, that may be," he continued. "But I think you look like you know what you're doing. When I was in high school at a little town called Parker, the girls never had the chance to play. I think it's great they do now, and I know I'm glad my own two girls will get that chance. If you like the game, you ought to play it."

"Maybe," she said. "But our junior high program has been so bad the last few years that we're becoming the doormats of the league. We play in the Black Hills Conference, and everyone else really beats up on us. Besides, I didn't like the coach, so I didn't go out."

Andrea looked over at him and shrugged. "I know you said there would be a new coach, but I might not like him, either. The coaching is really bad in the seventh and eighth grade. They just pick up anyone they can find so they can keep the girls' program going and have a team—like the law says they have to."

Forrest stopped and stared at her.

"That's a pretty impressive observation for a thirteen-year-old," he said. "Why do you think that?"

"My mom works over at the school. She's heard some of the coaches talk about putting up with this stupid junior high girls' sports stuff just so they can keep their own programs going. Then they complain about the varsity not having good teams. But how can they expect the varsity to get any better if they have lousy programs in junior high?"

"You're right," Forrest said. "But maybe they just haven't found the right coach yet. The new eighth-grade coach could turn things around if he's dedicated enough, and I know he'd be happy to have you on the team."

"How do you know?"

"Because it's going to be me."

Forrest gave her a little grin and broke back into a jog as they turned into the high school parking lot on the start back toward town. Andrea stood staring at him, then hurried to catch up. She caught him just as they passed the corner of the high school building and turned down the driveway leading past the school automotive shop.

A couple of high school boys and an older man were working there on the motor of a car, and a pretty, copper-haired girl was dribbling and shooting a basketball at a playground hoop nearby. They all looked up as the duo approached, and the girl stopped and nodded to Andrea.

Andrea forced a smile, then watched as the girl dribbled the ball quickly to the basket and hit a nice lay-up shot.

Forrest nodded and panted. "Now, that's not bad shooting. She one of the high school players?"

"Nope. That's Tracey LeDoux," Andrea panted in reply.

"She's in junior high. Eighth grade, like me."

"Really! A member of the team?"

They ran past them and Tracey took the ball out into the area near the free throw line and nailed a jump shot.

"No. She's sort of a loner. Stays around her boyfriend, John, a lot. He's the dark-haired one by the car. He's a junior already." She tried to keep the contempt out of her voice as she spoke, but it apparently came through anyway, she thought, because of the odd look Forrest gave her.

He stopped again and stood panting, the sun at his back and beads of perspiration on his forehead.

"You sound like you don't approve."

"I dunno." Andrea scuffed at the ground. "She's okay, I guess. But she seems like she's acting a little too old if you ask me. She's always hanging around him—never seems to have time to talk with any of the kids in our class."

Forrest watched as Tracey hit another driving lay-up, took down the rebound, and then swished a hook shot.

"Any of you try to talk to her first?" he asked. "Maybe she stays around John because you make her feel different. Maybe she stays around him because she doesn't have anything better to do." He grinned at her. "Like play basketball on a team, for example. If you don't mind, I think I'm going back to ask her about that. Want to come along?"

Andrea hesitated, and then shook her head.

"I—I think I'd better be heading back home, so Mom won't worry," she said. "You go ahead. Thanks for jogging with me." She turned away.

"Andrea!"

She stopped at his voice.

"I was serious about you coming out. If this team is in as sad shape as it sounds, I'm going to need some good players like you. You think about it some more. Please?"

She gave him a troubled smile, waved, and watched as he jogged back to where Tracey was shooting.

Now she had a problem. Playing for Coach Forrest would probably be okay, and she loved basketball. But not only she, but most of the other girls really didn't like Tracey. And if Tracey joined the team, maybe that was still reason enough not to play.

2
Talk About Tracey

School opened on a bright, sunny day. The hallways were jammed with laughing, shouting kids—the eighth graders confident and cool, the sixth graders nervous and lost.

"Feels sort of weird being oldest," Andrea said as she and Jill walked down the hallway toward their opening class.

"Yeah, I know," Jill answered, "but it's kind of nice being on top." She whispered loudly as several sixth graders walked past. "Those sixth graders look so little! Do you suppose we ever looked as jerky as they do?"

Someone gave her a shove from behind. "What do you mean, *did*? We grew up, Jill. *You* still look the same!"

It was tall, blonde, Betsy Pringle doing the talking, accompanied by Paula DeYoung and Lara Miller. Betsy was the class clown and also one of Andrea's favorite friends. She had been gone out of town for nearly a month, and Andrea squealed with happiness at seeing her again. They hugged each other while Jill gave Betsy a feigned look of disgust.

"Ho, ho, Pringle. Very funny. I see you brought the other two members of the triplets with you."

Betsy, Paula, and Lara did almost everything together. Like Betsy, Paula was slender and tall, but Lara was small and so thin she looked frail in comparison.

"Besides," Jill added, gesturing toward Lara, "*she* never grew up either, you know."

14

"Yeah, but at least I added some brains," Lara retorted.

"Hey, watch it, or I'll flatten you, you little shrimp!" Jill said. Her voice had taken on a tone that was more than joking. "And I don't even care if you've got a bad leg."

Lara was wearing a brace on her left knee from a muscle disease, which had caused her to leave school late in the spring and spend much of the summer at a rehabilitation hospital.

"My leg won't get in the way, so don't let that stop you from trying!" she snapped.

"Hey, come on, you two," Andrea intervened. "This is the first day of school, not the first day of the next world war." She grabbed Jill by the shoulders and pointed her back down the hall. "If we don't get our bodies into class, though, the teachers *will* start a war—with us."

Andrea had hoped her friend would have dropped some of her blustery ways in favor of being more agreeable—as she was apparently trying to do with the boys. But it looked like Jill was off to a bad start for the new year after all.

By noon the excitement of the first day was wearing off. Heavy homework had been handed out in two classes, and already everyone was grumbling in the lunchroom.

Andrea noticed Tracey in the lunch line and was surprised when she said hello. Tracey went to sit by herself at a corner table, and Andrea got her second surprise when Matt and two of his friends went to sit with her.

"Oh, no, now she's going to go after them." Andrea turned at the voice and found herself facing Patty Cordova.

"Huh?"

"Oh, that Tracey LeDoux," Patty replied. "You'd think she'd be happy lording it over us with her older boyfriend without trying to get all the guys from our class, too."

Patty and Tracey had been together on the cheerleading squad last year, but like the other girls in the class, Patty turned up her nose at Tracey dating a junior.

"Ummm, yeah," Andrea said with a sinking feeling as she watched Matt and Tracey share a laugh over something Matt had said. "Well, let's hope not."

Andrea joined Jill and several other girls at a center table. By the time they finished eating, Tracey's table was empty.

The afternoon classes seemed to drag, but it was not just because of the noon episode. Two sessions were in math and science—neither of which were her favorites—and home-work assignments in there seemed doubly hard.

As she walked back toward her locker, Andrea noticed the announcement about girls' basketball practice beginning the next day. It was right next to the one about any interested eighth graders coming out right after school to look into joining the cross-country team.

By three o'clock—just before the bell—she had made up her mind. She would go over to cross-country today, then check out the first basketball practice tomorrow. If Tracey showed up, she'd probably stick with running.

The cross-country coach had them get into lots of work right away, including calisthentics and a five-mile run. By the time she got back home and ate supper, she was exhausted, and her homework looked mountainous.

By 8:30, she had most of the homework completed. She grabbed a glass of milk and walked into the living room, where Mom was watching television. Andrea and her mother had lived alone since her dad died when she was six.

Her mother looked up and gave her a warm smile. "Hi. Got your homework all done?"

Andrea nodded.

"I don't know if I'll ever really understand math, though," she said after a sip of milk. "Did you have trouble with it when you were in school?"

"Sure," her mother chuckled. "Why do you think the banker keeps coming by to have those little talks with me?"

"I thought it was because he found someone pretty to talk to," Andrea quipped. Her mother rolled her eyes, and Andrea laughed. The new banker *had* been calling on her mother, and Andrea liked him. He'd even sat behind them in church last Sunday, and since he didn't regularly go to their church, Andrea saw some romantic meaning to that.

"Did you come in here to talk about me, or you?" her mother said, changing the subject. "I can tell when you've got that 'I need to talk' look in your eyes, so we'd better talk. You've got to get to bed, you know. School starts early, and now with the running, too, you need your rest."

"That's what I want to talk about. The running. I'm thinking about going out for basketball instead."

"Good." Her mother beamed. "Your dad would've been happy. He loved basketball."

Andrea smiled at her mother's enthusiasm.

"I'm just not real sure about it, though. The new coach is that Mr. Forrest who's teaching my Sunday school class."

"I thought you liked him."

"Oh, I do. That's not it. It's just that—when he talked to me about joining the team, he also talked to Tracey, and—"

"Tracey? Tracey LeDoux? That pretty little girl who lives on the farm out east of town?"

"Yeah. But she's not so little anymore. You're right, though, she *is* pretty. She's got this boyfriend who's a junior, and sometimes she makes the rest of us sick with the way she acts around him. She's only an eighth grader."

"Yes, I see," her mother said thoughtfully. "I hope you'll be holding off on any boyfriends yourself for a couple of years. I've been noticing the way you look at that Matt Polovich, and I get a little worried."

"Oh, Mom. Matt's just a friend. Tracey and John, well . . . it's kind of turned everyone off to her. Last summer, Jill tried to say something to her about it, and Tracey acted like Jill was some kind of baby or something—at least that's what Jill said. I wasn't there."

"So you think if Tracey's on the team, you two can't play together?"

"Yeah, sort of. I think it'll get everyone on the team upset if she goes around acting like she's older than the rest of us."

"Maybe she just needs a few of you to start being friends with her again," her mother said. "Maybe if she joins the team, she'll find out she can be friends with you girls and not have to act whatever way it is she acts around her boyfriend."

"Well, maybe. I just don't know."

Andrea's mother reached out and took her daughter's hands in hers. "Remember how you didn't like Jill because of her bad language and because she was such a tomboy?"

Andrea smiled and nodded.

"Well, you decided to be her friend, and now look. She's going to Sunday school, she has more friends, and you two are inseparable. You were good for her, but she did some things for you, too. Right?"

"Yeah, but—"

"Look, I'm not saying you have to be Tracey's friend. But maybe if she joins the team, she'll change some and so will each of you. And you could ask God to help you understand Tracey better. Besides, if you like basketball and you like the coach, you shouldn't let someone else decide whether or not you're going to play. Just go out and have fun."

Andrea gave her mother a hug. "Thanks, Mom. I'll try. Besides, maybe Tracey won't even come out."

She had no trouble at all getting to sleep that night, and her dreams were about making the winning basket from deep in the bushes.

Classes the next day seemed to drag, but as three o'clock approached, she had a bad case of butterflies in her stomach.

The locker room was buzzing, and she and the other girls hurried to change into gym clothes. Andrea noticed that there weren't many girls going to try out. In fact, counting her, there were only seven. Tracey was not there.

As the girls ran onto the court, Andrea saw Forrest give her a pleased smile, then look around at the others. His smile turned to a small frown, and it was apparent that he, too, was looking for Tracey. Then he smiled again and started tossing basketballs to the girls for them to take warm-up shots.

Andrea looked around at her teammates. Besides herself and Jill, there were the Triplets—Betsy, Paula, and Lara; Patty; and Arnell Longfellow. Arnie had moved to Sturgis from Rapid City and had played quite a bit on the seventh-grade team. Now, however, she looked out of shape.

Paula, who normally wore contacts, had on heavy athletic glasses. Andrea hadn't thought of her as being athletic, but Paula was making some moves inside which showed she had developed a lot of basketball skill over the summer. Lara, too, despite a complicated-looking brace on her left knee, seemed to be handling the ball well.

Andrea bounced the ball a few times and took some shots beside Jill, who ran about with reckless abandon, and sometimes sprawling on the floor after taking off-balance shots.

18

After about ten minutes, the coach called them together at mid-court and told them to sit down.

"My name is Tom Forrest," he began. "Most of you don't know me, but I know a couple of you." He smiled at Jill and Andrea. "This is my first coaching job, but I've played basketball and been part of it my whole life.

"When I was a junior and senior, my team went to the state tournament, and I played at guard. My teammates called me 'Tree.' " He paused. "I know, dumb name, but it goes with Forrest. Right?" The girls laughed.

"Of course, it's even dumber since I'm only five foot nine. But what I'm trying to get across is that you don't have to be big to be a good player and get a chance to play in the big tournaments.

"My family and I are new here in town, and I volunteered to coach you because I want to help get the girls' program turned around. The success of girls' basketball in Sturgis will start *right here*! If we build a winning attitude this year, it'll carry over to high school with you for the next four years. And the younger girls will want to do well, too."

Jill raised her hand, and he nodded to her.

"Don't you think it's going to be hard for us? We only won two games last year, and two of our starters are gone."

"Sure it is, but with hard work and *teamwork*, I think we can do okay. I see we have a little height, and a couple of you apparently have done some work this summer. Any of you go to basketball camp?"

Paula raised her hand, and Andrea nodded knowingly. Lara started to raise her hand, but stopped. Forrest pointed to her anyway.

"Well, not exactly a camp," she said. "I had to have some treatment for my left leg, and one of the therapists had me work out every day. We played a lot of basketball."

"Good. Everything you've done will be a plus for the team. Now, I don't know all of you by name yet, but I will by tomorrow. I had hoped we'd have a few more girls, but we'll just have to do the best we can with who we have."

Patty raised her hand. "My friend Michelle Mathers wants to come out, but she was afraid she wouldn't get much chance to play."

"Listen," Forrest said. "Every girl who comes out and works hard in practice will play in the games. We're going to be a team, and everyone on the team plays unless she gives me a good reason not to put her in. Okay?"

They all nodded.

"I've heard we may have a transfer student over from Douglas, but I don't know for sure. And I've talked with one other girl, so we'll see."

Tracey, thought Andrea. For the well-being of the team, she hoped Tracey's mind was made up, and her nonappearance was the final decision.

"Now, let's get to work," the coach said. "We'll be doing a lot of conditioning these first few days, and we'll start on plays by Monday. Our first game is two weeks from today, and I'll have a schedule for you tomorrow."

Clapping, the girls got to their feet and went through warm-up drills under Forrest's watchful eye. They followed that with wind sprints, and with running drills like three-man-weave and lay-ups. By five o'clock, they were beat, and there was little locker room talk as they showered and prepared for home.

As Andrea and Jill walked toward the gym door, Forrest stopped them.

"Glad you two are on the team," he said. "I was encouraged by the hustle you showed out here tonight. I think if we could pick up a couple more players, we might have a respectable team."

"You think we'll get any others?" Jill asked.

"Yes. Patty said her friend Michelle would be out, and I'm pretty sure we'll get that girl from Douglas. Then there's Tracey."

Jill looked startled. "Tracey LeDoux?"

"Yes."

"Oh." She said it quickly, then said nothing more. Forrest looked from her to Andrea with a question mark written on his face. Andrea gave a little shrug, but added nothing.

"Well, listen," he said, breaking the uncomfortable silence. "I have to get going. We'll see you two tomorrow, and by then we'll have some schedules to share, too." He waved and left the gym.

Jill turned quickly to face Andrea.

"Is he serious? Tracey! Why would he want her? Has she been throwing her body at him to get him interested?"

"Jill, that's not fair, and you know it. I think he wants her on the team because she's a good basketball player. I saw her shooting, and she looks pretty good.

"Besides, maybe if she played ball with us she'd forget all this 'grown-up' stuff and just act her age again."

"I doubt it," Jill snorted in disgust. "She thinks she's so sexy, running around with a junior. I can't believe her folks let her dress and act the way she does."

"She doesn't dress *sexy*," Andrea said, wondering suddenly why she was defending the girl she didn't like very much, either. Maybe it was her mother's talk from the night before.

"You sound like you're her best friend or something," Jill said sharply.

"No, I'm not her best friend at all. I've just been thinking about her lately, and I don't know if we've given her much of a chance. Maybe we're all just jealous 'cause she's got a boyfriend and we don't."

"Yeah, well, it looks like maybe you're getting one yourself."

Andrea glared at her friend. "If you mean Matt, you're crazy. I keep telling you, we're just friends. Besides, what's that got to do with anything? We don't even know if Tracey's going to come out. And, if she does, all I'm saying is that she should have a chance."

Jill said nothing, turning instead toward the door and stomping out. Andrea watched her for a few seconds, then grabbed her gym bag and started to follow. But Jill was nowhere in sight when Andrea reached the door.

If this was the way things were going to be by adding Tracey, maybe it *would* be for the best if she didn't show up. Andrea couldn't remember when she'd seen Jill so *really* mad. She knew some of the rest of the girls might consider quitting the team if Tracey joined. If Coach Forrest really hoped to build a winning team with a great attitude, he should think twice about adding Tracey LeDoux.

It might hurt more than help to have her on the team.

21

3
New Girl in Town

On Friday, the team size grew by two as Patty's friend Michelle Mathers joined the team, and the transfer student Coach Forrest had spoken about showed up for practice.

Her name was Courtney Smith and her dress and appearance made her stand out immediately. Her clothes were tight fitting and she wore lots of makeup. Normally she would have been at Douglas, the air force base school, but her dad had wanted to live away from the base.

Courtney, at five foot seven, had the size to be a forward, and she came onto the practice floor with confidence and some obvious skill. In the locker room, she chatted easily with the other girls. For being in a new school for her first day, she didn't appear even a bit nervous.

Andrea noticed that most of her conversation was about boys—either those she had known or those she had seen today. She also noticed that Jill seemed to be going out of her way to be friends with Courtney. It really bugged her. She felt like Jill was doing it just to get even with her for sticking up for Tracey.

As they went to pick up the basketballs, Jill stopped Andrea.

"Courtney's cool," she said.

"A little heavy on the makeup, don't you think?" Andrea snapped.

"No. I think it's great. She's going to show me how to use more makeup, too. I like her style."

She gave Andrea a look of defiance and then ran over to join her new friend. Andrea felt a rush of jealousy. She'd hate to lose Jill. She shouldn't have snapped at her.

She knew Jill was still mad about the Tracey talk—and just about Tracey. Besides calling Jill a baby, Tracey had, Jill claimed, called her "boyish," and Jill had wanted to fight because of it. The thing was, Jill *had* been acting like a boy—especially when she wanted to fight all the time. Now, instead of acting "boyish," she was acting boy crazy.

And Courtney was a friend who wasn't going to make that situation any better.

Practice went well and the team worked on a lot of three-on-two's and three-man-weave, the former drill sending three offensive players against two on defense, and the latter providing the chance to pass the ball and "weave" quickly upcourt in the process.

The coach closed out the session with some line drills with the basketball, having each girl dribble to the free throw line and back, to half court and back, to the opposite free throw line and back, and finally full court and back.

After twice through the line drills, they were all gasping and perspiring. Forrest sent them to the free throw lines for ten free throws apiece. Then he sat them down.

"Okay," he said, waving a stack of papers at them, "here's our schedule. We've got fourteen games—twelve against conference teams, and two nonconference against St. Martin's and Rapid City North." He paused as the girls groaned.

"I know, I know," he said. "North is probably the biggest and best eighth-grade team in our area, but the game will be good experience. We play every conference team once and the five closest to us twice. These are the schools you'll be playing all through high school, so now's the time to develop a winning tradition against them."

He passed out the schedule sheets, and Andrea scanned her copy. It showed the opening game at home against Custer on September 20, and then games twice a week through November 6 when they closed with North.

They would play Custer and Hot Springs—the two

Southern Hills members of the conference—only once each. The longest road trip would be to Hot Springs, about an hour-and-a-half drive.

In the locker room, the talk alternated between the upcoming schedule and plans for the weekend.

"What's the main action around here on Saturdays?" Courtney asked as she paused in front of the mirror to check her lipstick and brush at her hair.

"Not much for kids our age," Paula said. "Maybe once we get a little more into the school year we can set up a trip to Rapid or something."

"What about partying?" Courtney asked as she turned toward the bench where Andrea was dressing. "Where's the party action?"

Andrea glanced at Paula and they both smiled.

"Afraid we don't have much of that," she said. "We've got the theater and roller-skating. Usually our moms won't let us get into parties with the older kids. Guess they think we're a little young yet."

Courtney looked around the room with amazement.

"I can't believe you just sit around and do nothing. Girls, you've got to make your own action if nothing is available. Where do the high school guys hang out?"

"It's a place called the White Rabbit," Jill piped up.

"Well, why don't we go over there tomorrow night and check out some of those guys?"

The room grew quiet until Jill spoke again.

"I might go with you. Could be fun."

"Jill, your mom won't let you go over to the Rabbit, and you know it," Andrea said. "Why even think about—"

"I can go over there if I want to! Why does my mom have to know about it? Unless you're planning to tell her?" She said it with a challenge in her voice, and Andrea shook her head.

"No, I'm not going to tell her. I just don't think you should go. Besides, Courtney, your mom probably wouldn't want you over there, either. It's mostly for the older high school kids and some of those who already graduated. Some of us were talking about taking in the movie. Why don't we all just go there, instead?"

"Thanks, but no thanks," Courtney replied. "I think this

White Rabbit place sounds just right. I haven't got a mom, anyway, and my dad'll be working. He wouldn't care." She turned back to Jill. "You coming, too?"

Jill looked quickly around the room at her classmates, then nodded. "You bet. Maybe someone else will be ready to go with us by then, too." She picked up her gym bag and walked over to Courtney's side. "If you want to join in the *action*," she said, looking back, "call me at home tomorrow. Courtney and I are going to talk over our plans."

They exited together.

"They won't go," Patty said with a halfhearted laugh. "Besides, the guys I want to 'check out' are the ones in our class who are going to the movie. That's where you'll find me tomorrow night." Patty brushed back her long, dark hair and tied it up with a bright blue ribbon as she spoke.

The others laughed, and they left the locker room laughing and talking together about what a dumb idea it was for Courtney and Jill to think they could fit in at the Rabbit. But underneath, Andrea knew they were probably as worried as she was that the girls would actually do it.

She'd call Jill in the morning and get things stopped before her friend got herself in trouble with her parents by doing something stupid.

Andrea fidgeted over her homework that night and thought several times about going to the phone to call Jill. Each time, though, she hesitated because she didn't want her mother to hear the conversation. Finally, she decided to wait until morning when her mother would be out.

She slept fitfully, woke several times with a nightmare about Jill getting into trouble, and finally fell into a deep sleep about four. When she woke, it was past nine-thirty.

Her mother had left for a club meeting, and a note on the kitchen table reminded Andrea to take a bag of sewing materials to a neighbor's house and to get a casserole ready for an early evening dinner. The banker, Jack Ramsey, would be coming for dinner, and then he and her mother were going into Rapid City to a play.

Andrea gulped a bowl of cereal, washed up, then dialed Jill's number. Jill's mother answered.

"Hi, Mrs. B.," she said cheerily. "Jill there?"

"Why no, Andrea, I'm sorry. She went over to her new friend's house. You know, that new girl on the basketball team—Courtney. Courtney called and asked her to come over today and then spend the night. Do you want the telephone number?"

"Uh, no. No, thanks, Mrs. B. I'm sorry I missed her. I kinda slept in this morning, or I would've called earlier. Do you know where Courtney lives? I might just go over and say hello. I should get to know Courtney better, too."

"Why, yes. They're living in the old Jackson house on Eighth. You know where that's at, don't you?"

"Yes. Thanks. Bye." Andrea hung up and wondered what to do next. She wanted to get on her bike and go right over to Courtney's. But she also didn't want Jill to think she was trying to tell her what to do. Their friendship was shaky enough right now. Finally, she decided to take the sewing materials to the neighbor's, then ride to Patty's house. Maybe together they could go past Courtney's place and make it look like something that wasn't planned.

Patty lived on Sixth, only a few blocks from the Jackson place, and she and Michelle were in the front yard practicing cheerleading yells when Andrea rode up.

Patty was dark and very pretty and trim. She always kept her raven black hair tied back or in ponytails with bright ribbons. She loved cheerleading and had been the captain for the seventh-grade unit, which cheered at the boys' games.

Michelle was blonde and lanky and had her hair cut short. She was as uncoordinated as Patty was coordinated, and looked almost comical working with Patty on the cheerleading routines.

The girls stopped and walked over to join Andrea as she laid down her bike. Michelle grinned, and the sun glinted off a row of braces.

"Hi," Patty said. "Me 'n' Michelle are working on my cheerleading drills. I want to get started early so I'll be ready when the tryouts come up for the boys' season. I figure being on the basketball team will help get me in shape faster."

"You won't have any problems," Andrea said. "Everybody knows you're the best cheerleader in the school."

Patty grinned. "Maybe. But I don't want to miss out on being captain again. And Michelle heard that Tracey LeDoux's going to be trying out again, and I'd hate to have *her* get the captain's spot."

That was another little battle that had put Tracey on the outside, Andrea remembered. Tracey and Patty had both been on the cheerleading squad, and some of the kids had told Patty that they thought Tracey should have been the captain instead of Patty.

"Tracey's cute, but I'm going to show her I'm a better cheerleader than she is," Patty added. She tossed her head indignantly and did a quick cartwheel to make her point.

Both Michelle and Andrea applauded the effort.

"When it comes to boys, though, you're *way* behind," Michelle said. "She's got *John,* and you better not forget it!"

"Big deal!" Patty said with a laugh. "I think I can do just fine with the boys when I'm ready to. Hey, maybe we should try to get Tracey together with old Courtney. Now there's a girl who can tell Courtney where to find the action!"

The girls laughed, but Andrea didn't, and they gave her a questioning look.

"Speaking of Courtney. Have you seen her or Jill yet today?" she asked.

They shook their heads.

"I guess Jill is over at her house and is going to stay there tonight. They only live a couple blocks from here."

"Good grief!" Patty said. "You don't think Jill's actually going to go with her to the Rabbit, do you? They're both going to be in big trouble if they get caught over there."

"That's what I was thinking, too," Andrea said. "I thought maybe we could kinda ride by there and if we see them, try to talk them into doing something with us tonight, instead. What do you guys think?"

"Sure, why not?" Patty said with a shrug. "I think Courtney's all talk anyway, and you know Jill. She's just showing off to impress Courtney."

They hopped on their bikes and made the quick trip over to Eighth. The place looked deserted, but they tried the bell anyway. There was no answer.

"Maybe they went downtown," Michelle said.

They wheeled down to Main Street and made a couple of quick stops at the usual junior high hangouts, but the girls were not anywhere to be found. Andrea went back to Patty's and had lunch there, then made the whole route alone one more time—with the same results.

Back at home, she started the casserole, then called the Bradford home once more. This time, she asked for Courtney's phone number and gave it a try. By four-thirty, when her mother arrived, she had tried half a dozen times without success. Now she would have to wait until after dinner when her mother and Mr. Ramsey left for Rapid.

The dinner went quickly, and Andrea almost forgot about the plight of her friend in the presence of the banker, who kept her laughing with his stories. She noticed again how often he looked with admiration at her mother, and how happy Mom seemed in his company. "Jack," as he told her to call him, paid plenty of attention to Andrea, too, asking her about school, her hobbies, and the basketball team.

By the time the dishes were done and the adults had left for the play, it was nearly seven o'clock. The movie started at seven-thirty. Andrea tried Courtney's place again and still got no answer; then she ran outside as a horn sounded. Patty's dad was driving them to the theater.

"Find them?" Patty asked as she climbed into the backseat.

Andrea shook her head.

"Well, don't worry. Sometimes Jill acts stupid, but she won't do anything to get herself in trouble."

The movie was a comedy, and a good one, but despite that Andrea couldn't stop thinking about Jill being gone. Patty was probably right, but she wondered where the two girls had disappeared to.

As they walked out of the theater, a car drove past and honked several times. Andrea recognized the driver as a senior who she had heard some bad things about.

"Andrea! Hi!"

She looked at the car again at the sound of her name and suddenly felt sick. Leaning out the back window and shouting and waving to her was Courtney. Sitting next to her was Jill.

28

4
Sky Hook

Andrea went to Sunday school fully expecting not to see Jill. But she had her second major surprise in two days when her friend slipped into the classroom just as Coach Forrest was beginning the lesson.

Jill looked tired, but she smiled triumphantly at Andrea before taking an empty chair near the door. Several times during the lesson the girls exchanged glances, but each time one of them immediately looked away.

When the class ended, Andrea jumped up and followed Jill, who was already on her way out. But Matt stopped her and asked about the movie. By the time Andrea got into the hallway, Jill was nowhere to be seen.

"Walk you to the door?" Matt said, returning to her side. Andrea nodded.

"You and Jill have a fight or something?" he asked.

"Why?"

"Because you're almost always together, and last night she wasn't with you, and now today she left right away."

"Yeah, well, I guess a little fight," Andrea said. "She found another new friend, too. That new girl. Courtney."

"Sure, I saw her Friday," Matt said. "She talked to quite a few of the guys. Everyone was surprised at how she acted."

They walked around the corner and almost ran into Jill and two other girls. Jill raised her voice when she saw Andrea.

29

"And it was a blast!" she said. "Those guys took us over to the Rabbit, then all the way down to Rapid and back. Courtney's great, because she knew exactly how to act with them. She's a really neat friend."

Andrea stopped. "Hi, Jill," she said. "Sorry I missed you yesterday. I was hoping we could talk, you know?"

"Yeah, well, maybe some other time," Jill said. "I gotta go now because Courtney's coming by my place after lunch. Too bad you couldn't have come with us last night. Maybe your friend Tracey can take you out on the town with her and John sometime." She smirked and walked away.

"What was that all about?" Matt asked.

"Oh, nothing. Really. She got mad at me in the first place because I said maybe we ought to give Tracey a chance to be friends. She's been mad at Tracey for months. It's just stupid, that's all!"

"Yeah, that's for sure," Matt said. "Besides, I agree with you. I like Tracey. Everybody talks about her and John, but I don't think it's so bad. John's a nice guy, and he and Tracey are both pretty nice as far as I can tell."

Andrea gave him a surprised look. "I didn't even know you knew him."

"Yeah. He's a friend of my brother. I thought it was kind of weird for him to start dating an eighth grader, but they're not doing anything wrong. Anyway, she's a year older than the rest of us because her folks started her late in school."

"I didn't know that, either. I guess there's a lot about her and John that most of us don't know."

"Well, sit down and talk with her sometime," Matt answered. "You girls always leave her alone at school, so some of the guys have been asking her to eat lunch with us. She's really nice."

Andrea nodded. Matt was right. Maybe it was time to get to know Tracey better, and she'd be the one to try first.

At school the next day, she looked for Tracey and then sat down beside her in the cafeteria.

"Hi."

Tracey looked up in surprise as Andrea sat down, then nodded. "Hi." She went back to eating. She chewed a mouthful of peas and carrots, glanced at Andrea again, then spoke. "You lost or something?"

"No. I came here to eat with you."

"How come?"

"I wanted to ask you to join our basketball team."

"Why? I thought all the girls hated me."

"They don't hate you. They're just jealous because you've got a boyfriend and they don't." Andrea stirred her fork through her own vegetables as she spoke. "Anyway, I've been thinking that maybe we haven't given you a chance to be our friend, so—"

"So you want me to be on your team so that I can make friends."

Andrea turned a little red. "Well, not exactly. I saw you shooting that day, too, you know. We need you on the team because you play pretty good basketball."

Tracey stared at her, and then burst into laughter.

"I'll think about it," she responded. "But don't be surprised if I'm not there when practice starts. Okay?"

"Okay. But think about it hard. We really do need you on the team. And I just know you'll make some friends, too."

Andrea started eating, and Tracey finished up in silence. She stood and pulled back her tray, then sat down again.

"Look, if I decide to come out, everybody'll probably just be on my case. That's not going to help the team at all."

"Maybe," Andrea answered. "But maybe some of the girls will get to know you a little better, and then we can all be friends again. I know you've always sort of kept to yourself, but I think we were all friends last year before you started going out with John."

"Well, I never wanted to stop having any of the girls as friends. Everybody just stopped talking to me after I started going out with him."

Andrea went back to stirring her food before saying anything more.

"Look, why don't you just give the team a try for a week or two and see what happens. Okay? I want to be your friend again, and you know the coach wants you there. Everybody else'll change, too, if you give 'em a chance."

Tracey stood up again and forced a smile. "If you see me in

the locker room, I'll be coming out. If not, I won't. Okay?"

Andrea nodded.

"And if I don't, can we still be friends?"

"Sure. Especially if you'll help me with my math." Andrea grinned, and Tracey laughed and walked away.

Well, step one was completed and had seemed to go okay, she thought as she carried her tray to the return window. If Tracey did decide to come out, though, step two wouldn't be so easy.

At practice time, Tracey was not there, and Andrea's heart sank at her failure. She shot half-heartedly at the basket and was about to toss the ball aside when Patty ran over and grabbed her arm.

"I don't believe it!"

"What?" She glanced in the direction Patty was pointing. Coming into the gym with a bag in her left hand was Tracey. Andrea gasped slightly, then smiled.

"Can you believe it?" Patty said in disgust. "First I gotta put up with her in cheerleading, and now she's coming out for basketball, too. I don't believe it!"

Coach Forrest walked over and gave Tracey a warm pat on the shoulder, pointed toward the locker room, and then gestured back toward the court. All the girls had stopped shooting and were staring at the coach and his new recruit.

"Well, Andrea, looks like you got your wish," Jill said snidely as she walked over to join Andrea and Patty. "Looks like she's already got the coach wrapped around her little finger, so she'll have a starting-five spot wrapped up, too."

"Oh, shut up, Jill!" Andrea said quickly. "He's just glad to see her out, and so am I. I know she can shoot well, but who knows how she'll do with the team? The least we can do is give her a chance."

"Why?" Patty asked. "I don't like her. I never have and I never will."

"Because of her boyfriend?"

"No. Because she's always so snobby. She never has time for anyone else, and she always thinks she's better than everyone."

"She's just quiet and keeps to herself a lot,"

Andrea said, suddenly feeling that this talk was going nowhere but downhill. "I just think we should give her a chance."

Andrea was about to say something further when the coach blew his whistle and motioned them to start three-on-two's. A few minutes later, Tracey jogged out onto the court to join them. Forrest said a few words to her and then motioned for her to join the drill.

"Come on, Tracey, fit in," Andrea muttered to herself. She closed her eyes tightly for a few seconds and prayed that the other girls would accept Tracey. She opened them, saw Tracey looking her way, and smiled. Tracey returned the smile, and then they were off and running on a three-on-two with no time to worry about what would come next.

Practice went well. Coach Forrest introduced the team to the first play he wanted them to learn—The Wheel. It was a play designed for use against a man-to-man defense where each girl away from the ball would roll across the free throw lane like they were on the edge of a wheel. As she crossed the lane, each girl would be looking for a pass and then be expected to take the ball into the basket to shoot.

It was a fun play, and after two or three times when the girl getting the pass actually scored a basket, they were all laughing and cheering for each other. Jill pulled up beside Andrea waiting her turn to go into the wheel rotation. She applauded when Paula took the ball and scored, and then spoke to Andrea as if forgetting about their ongoing argument.

"Man, this is great! We never had a play like this last year with old Donohue. And I think we're handling the ball better, too. This guy's a good coach."

Andrea nodded. "I don't know what else we're going to learn, but I think we're doing okay, so far."

"You were right about Tracey, too," Jill added grudgingly. "She's a good shooter. . . . But I still don't like her!" she continued. "As long as she does things for the team, I'll play with her. But I won't be her friend." Jill took off, elbowed her way past Michelle and shot hard off the backboard, missing the shot by a couple of feet. Then she took the ball outside and rifled a pass back to Andrea.

The ball came to her so hard it stung her fingers, but Andrea clenched her teeth, dribbled across the lane, and shot a sweeping hook shot which bounced around the rim and then fell in.

She clapped her stinging hands to show Jill nothing was wrong, then took her own place in the passing line as her teammates clapped and cheered.

"All right, Andrea!" Paula called. "Way to hit the sky hook."

Sky hook, Andrea thought. That's what she needed right now. A hook to come down out of the sky and pull Jill up and give her a good shaking. *Okay, God, reach down and do something to Jill.* If only it could be that easy.

By the sixth day into practice, the Scoopers had learned another play and were doing some serious work on team drills that would be used in their games. And already Andrea knew she was in a good spot to become a starting forward by the time the first game rolled around in less than a week.

It was apparent that Paula would be the starting center. Tracey and Courtney were almost dead even for the other forward spot, while Jill, Lara, and Patty were battling for the two guard positions.

No one but Andrea and the coach talked socially to Tracey, but the newest member of the team appeared not to care. And once the team was in scrimmage situations on the court, Tracey got her share of the passes and shots despite the team's open animosity toward her.

"They know that they better pass the ball to her and act like a team if they ever expect to play in a game for me," Forrest said when Andrea cornered him after practice to talk about Tracey. "I can make them pass her the ball, but I can't make them be her friend. And I don't understand it because she really seems like a nice girl."

"She is," Andrea said. "I've gotten to know her a little better these last few days, and now I wish we had been friends all along. I just worry about the way the rest of the team keeps treating her."

"Well, I'm glad you're worried, but I think if she has the guts to stick with it that eventually some of them will start talking to her," Forrest responded. "Meanwhile, I've noticed that a couple of them are a little down on you for taking Tracey's side."

Andrea wiped her brow and hung her head slightly.

"Yeah, I know, but I can handle it. Besides, I'm sure that both Jill and Patty will be my friends again after they get through this next week or so. I'm just worried that maybe I shouldn't have talked to Tracey about coming out. Maybe I'll just make it worse for her instead of better."

"Oh, so that's why she finally decided to come out," Forrest said. "I figured it wasn't just my nice, fatherly ways that convinced her."

Andrea laughed with him. "Yeah, like these nice, kind running drills you keep having us do. I didn't know dads could be so mean," she teased.

As the days passed and school got into a routine, Andrea found herself concerned with three things: how the basketball team was progressing, how hard the homework seemed to be, and how much farther apart she and Jill seemed to be getting.

Each school day, Jill was spending more and more time around Courtney, and now, like Courtney, Jill was wearing lots of makeup and slipping off with Courtney to join a group of older kids who cruised Main and the strip between the V.A. and the city in their cars. Andrea was wondering how her friend could be finding the time to do that, play basketball, and still get the homework completed—especially as hard as the math and science seemed to be getting.

On Friday, the eighth day of school, she made a point of finding Jill before school.

"You get your math problems done?" Andrea asked.

"A couple of them. Didn't have time for the rest."

"But we've got to turn this assignment in," Andrea said. "Aren't you worried about your grade?"

"It's early in the year. Even if I get a bad grade now, I'll have plenty of time to get it back up. I don't understand it, anyway. Maybe I'll just copy someone else's stuff."

They were walking slowly down the hall toward their lockers, and Andrea pulled up at the remark.

"You can't just cheat. How's that going to help you when we start getting quizzes and tests? Jill, you've got to quit messing around every day and night and start getting your studying done."

"Who says I'm messing around?" Jill demanded.

"No one. But you'd have to be blind not to see you and Courtney out riding around with those guys from the high school all the time."

Jill pulled a long-handled comb from her jeans pocket and combed twice at each side of her hair. Then she took out a small pocket mirror and looked at her eye shadow and lipstick. "You think I need a little touch-up on this one?" she asked, pointing to her left eye.

"No, I think you need a little touch-up on your brain," Andrea retorted. "You've got way too much makeup on already, and you're not studying enough to even keep yourself in school. Jill, don't be dumb enough to follow Courtney around like a puppy dog or something."

"You're just wishing she was your friend instead of mine," Jill replied. She started on toward her locker and Andrea walked along.

"Oh, give me a break," Andrea said sarcastically. Then she got serious again. "Look, I just want you to keep things right, that's all. And I want to be your friend again. Okay?"

"Sure, why not? But I'm not going to stop being Courtney's friend just to be yours."

"I didn't ask you to. All I'm saying is that you've always had to work just as hard as I have to keep your grades up, and if you don't start studying pretty soon you're going to flunk out. Then you'll have plenty of time to run around town."

They reached their lockers and stopped.

"I'm not going to flunk," Jill snapped as she yanked open her locker. "Now just leave me alone. Okay?"

"Sure, but—"

"Hey, there's Courtney now!" Jill interrupted, pointing down the hallway. "Look, I'll see you later. Gotta go now." She grabbed a couple of books from the locker, slammed the door shut, and hurried off down the hall as Andrea stared in frustration at her back.

5
Starting Five

Betsy, Lara, and Paula were whispering together in the corner of the locker room when Andrea walked in, but she ignored them and began getting changed. It was Wednesday night before the game, and she was too nervous to get involved in one of their little plots.

Betsy was forever coming up with one scheme or another to play a joke on someone in the class, and twice she had broken up practice with a prank on her teammates. Each time, Coach Forrest had made her run laps, but even he had joined in the laughter.

Tonight, though, would not be a good time for joking, Andrea decided. Coach Forrest would be naming the starting lineup for tomorrow night's game, and with this being youth group Bible study night, the practice would be short and to the point. She slipped on her practice jersey just as Jill and Courtney came in.

"Well, you guys ready?" she asked as Courtney stepped over to the mirror to check her hair.

"Sure, no sweat," Courtney answered. "You and I will be starting forwards, you know."

"What makes you say that?"

"Oh, come off it, Andrea," Jill said. "Everyone out there can see the coach likes you. You'll get to be a starter."

"And I'll be a starter because I'm better than the other

forwards," said Courtney. "Besides, I've been working harder at it than the others."

"And you don't think I have?" Andrea said indignantly. "Maybe the coach likes me, but I've been working as hard as anyone at practice. If I get a starting spot, it's because I've earned it!"

She stopped, her face flushed, and looked around the room. The other girls had stopped talking and were looking at them. Andrea looked at her shoes, yanked the laces tight, and headed out to the gym. She was angry as she grabbed a ball and began shooting, and her anger had only subsided some by the time the Triplets and Arnie came onto the floor to join her.

"Don't worry about it," Paula said. "They're just trying to get your goat. You've earned your spot."

Betsy nodded and glanced back at the locker room door. "And since Courtney thinks she's so hot, we fixed up a little something to help her cool off." She grinned and raced over to pick up a basketball just as the coach walked onto the floor.

Patty, Michelle, and Tracey came out. The locker room door was still closing when an ear-shattering shriek came from within. Betsy and Lara doubled over in laughter, and Paula stopped shooting momentarily to cover her mouth.

Forrest looked startled, then started toward the locker room. Jill came racing out.

"Coach! It's Courtney! She, uh—" She pointed back into the locker room, and then started to laugh herself.

"What is it? I better go in there. Is she dressed?"

Jill just nodded and pushed the door open so the coach could go in. A few seconds later he emerged. He had a slight grin on his face, too, but his expression sobered quickly, and he waved the team toward him.

"None of you would happen to know about that little gizmo that just dumped water all over Courtney, would you?" He looked directly at Betsy as he spoke.

"Science experiment," she mumbled. "Gee, I guess it must work."

He made a circling motion with his hand, and Betsy flipped her basketball to him and started to run.

"How many?" she shouted back over her shoulder.

"Five!" he shouted back. Then to the rest of the team he added, "I wish she could play basketball with as much effort as she puts into these pranks of hers." He waved back to the floor. "Come on, get on your shots and leave Courtney alone. Jill, go on back in and tell her she's got five more minutes to get fixed up and get out here."

Jill disappeared inside and they heard some muffled shouting. In a few seconds she returned.

"I think she wants more time, Coach. Her makeup and her hair—"

"I *know* what they look like," Forrest said. "I just saw her. Remember? Tell her five minutes. Everyone will love her just the way she is. After all, we're all friends here, right?" He held his arms wide and shrugged, then pointed to the floor. "Now start shooting!"

The rest of the team hurried to resume shooting, while Jill edged back into the locker room. She returned in less than a minute, giggling hard about Courtney looking "like a drowned rat." Then she got very serious. "But that thing coming out of her locker scared her half to death!" She looked hard at everyone for a few seconds, and then burst into giggles again.

The other girls started to laugh, too, but quickly resumed shooting as Forrest took some menacing steps in their direction.

At the end of five minutes, Courtney came onto the floor, her wet hair combed straight and the makeup around her eyes blotchy.

Forrest blew his whistle and called the team around him.

"All right. Tomorrow night we open with Custer. I don't know a lot about these teams yet, but I've been told that they're pretty tough and have a shot at the conference championship. I think we've been having some good practices and been looking pretty good, but it's hard to say how we're going to do until we play someone.

"Tonight, we're going to work on some pregame routines. We may or may not win a lot of games, but I want you to look sharp when you're warming up. Okay?"

They all nodded.

"Next item. I'd like to have a team prayer before each

game, but I'm going to leave it up to you guys. What do you think?"

Everyone was quiet for several seconds, then Courtney spoke up. "I think it's a real dumb idea."

Several of the other girls gasped, and Andrea felt her anger toward Courtney surge up again. She stared at Courtney's streaked face.

Forrest responded quietly. "How come?"

"Because prayer doesn't work, that's why. What works is bustin' your gut to get things done. My dad says that's the way to succeed, and he's doin' fine. Same thing's true for this team. We get out here and work hard, we'll win. If we don't, we'll lose. Simple as that."

Andrea flipped her hand up almost before she knew it.

"I think it'd be a good idea to pray," she said. "I agree with Courtney that we've got to work hard, but I like to ask God to give me the strength to do well. And it doesn't hurt to thank him for giving us the ability to play!"

Several of the others nodded.

Forrest held up a hand for quiet. "Okay, we'll have a vote. Who would be against a team prayer?"

Courtney raised her hand and looked around. Slowly, Jill also raised her hand. Andrea felt a sinking in her stomach at Jill's reaction.

"How many are for the prayer?"

The other eight girls raised their hands.

"Okay, it's 8-2 in favor. But I'm not going to force you two girls to participate in the prayer if you don't want to," Forrest said. "Okay?"

They both nodded.

"Now. Back to the game. We'll be starting out in a man-to-man defense and then if we have to we'll switch into a zone—probably that two-one-two we've been working with. Any questions on that?"

Arnie raised her hand, and Forrest pointed to her.

"In the two-one-two, the two forwards play underneath the basket and the center in the middle of the lane?"

"Right. And the two guards are up by the free throw line. But you don't just stand around in those spots and watch. You've got to play with your hands up all the time, and challenge the girl with the ball when she's in your area. But we may not even use the two-one-two. We're a fairly quick team, and I think we can stay with the other teams by playing man-to-man. Okay?"

Again, they all nodded.

"Now, at the end of practice I'll tell you who's going to be starting in the game tomorrow night. It's very close among some of you, so what you show me out here today will make the difference. So pay attention, do what I ask you, and we'll see how it goes."

The girls got to their feet, and Forrest held out his right hand. He paused.

"One more thing, girls. We're going into this season as a team. As long as you continue to work hard out here in practice, each of you plays. So, if you don't become a starter, don't get down on yourself or your teammates. Now, everybody put a hand in here and let's have a good practice!"

They all stacked their hands together on top of Forrest's, shouted "Teamwork!" then broke into two lines for lay-ups and the rest of the pregame drill. Fifty minutes later, after the drill and a twenty-minute "game" scrimmage, he blew the whistle again and called them back together.

"All right, I've made my decision on the starters. We'll have Andrea and Courtney at the forwards; Paula at center; and Jill and Lara at the guards."

Andrea looked at her teammates for their reaction. Courtney had an "I told you so" look on her face, and Tracey looked upset, but all the others, including Patty, were smiling and nodding.

The girls ran a team lap to close out the practice, then clambered into the locker room to hurry out and get home for various church events. Only Courtney seemed unconcerned about the time.

"I'm not going to any church here, anyway," she said when Paula asked. "Besides, I have a little extra time to spend in here, thanks to *someone*. I wouldn't be caught dead outside looking like this."

Andrea swallowed. She still felt mad at Courtney. But it wouldn't be right to let that get in the way of helping someone. Even Courtney. She decided to let her anger go.

"You can come and visit our church sometime," she volunteered. "I mean, if you're interested in finding a place."

Courtney looked surprised. "I dunno," she replied quickly. "We've never been much on going to church or anything like that. I don't even understand why you all go to these Wednesday night things."

"It's for youth group," Andrea said. "We learn more about the Bible and the church, and about ourselves and our friends. It's like a combination study and fun time." She paused and glanced at Courtney. Was there a faint flicker of interest on her face?

"Or, you could visit our Sunday school class some time," Andrea went on. She grinned. "I guess you know who teaches that."

Courtney started to nod—then shook her head. "Naw, maybe not. Like I said, we're not much on church, and my dad has to work some Sundays."

Andrea shrugged. "Okay, suit yourself. But you're always welcome." She started for the door, and then looked back. "Congratulations on making the starting five."

Courtney had walked to the mirror and was staring at herself and making a face. If she heard Andrea, she didn't acknowledge it.

"Yeah, well, you, too, Andrea," Andrea said softly to herself as she walked out into the gym and headed for home.

About a hundred people were in the stands when the girls came out of the locker room in their black and white game uniforms and got ready for the warm-up drills they had practiced the day before.

Andrea scanned the crowd, spotted her mother, and waved. Her mother, sitting next to Jill's mom, waved back. Then she was off and running through the lay-up drill.

The girls were fired up and ready to go. Forrest had said little to them before sending them onto the court. It was about twenty-five minutes to game time. Andrea made three straight lay-ups, and then missed. She stopped shooting and watched as the Custer Wildcats in their purple and gold uniforms raced out from the visitors' locker room and began their own warm-ups.

42

Tracey walked over to Andrea's side.

"They look pretty good," she said quietly. "And they've got so many more players than we do."

Andrea nodded as she watched a rangy red-haired girl dribble the ball behind her back and drive to the basket for a lay-up.

"Brother!" she exclaimed. "Did you see that?"

Some of the other Sturgis girls gasped, too, at the Custer girl's move. Paula clapped hands together and motioned toward their own basket.

"Come on, you guys, let's get with it! Quit worrying about them. Let's get our own team ready."

The other girls started clapping and talking to each other, and soon they were back into their own routine. Forrest walked onto the court, watched them for a few minutes, and then joined the Custer coach at mid-court. They stood watching the two teams and talking, and Andrea thought that twice they motioned in her direction.

With five minutes left, the teams both left for their locker rooms and the coaches shook hands.

Everyone was fidgeting nervously when Forrest walked into the room.

"Okay," he started. "They're good. We knew they'd be good, so that shouldn't come as too much of a surprise. After watching them warm up, though, I want us to come right out in a zone defense. They've got a couple of girls who are quicker than us, and it's not fair to expect one of you to try to stop one of them playing man to man.

"Now I know you're going to be nervous and you might miss a few shots early, but don't let that stop you from taking the open shots. If you're open and you're within your range, I want you to shoot. If you play good defense and get some of those shots to fall, we'll be okay.

"Any questions?"

The room grew dead silent.

"All right. Then we'll have our prayer and get back on the court. Go into free throws when you get back out there."

The girls gathered in a circle and clasped hands, and Andrea was pleased—and surprised—to see first Jill and then Courtney step into the circle and join in. They all bowed together. Forrest said a brief prayer, and then looked up.

"This is it," he said. They reached their hands together in the center of the circle. "Give it your best and let's get a victory."

They all shouted "Victory!" then broke out of the locker room and onto the floor with about two minutes left on the clock. The Custer girls were already there, and they, too, were shooting free throws. The buzzer sounded, and they gathered at the bench for last-second instructions.

Andrea looked to her mother again and was pleased to see Jack sitting behind her and Jill's mother. Just to their left, Matt and two of his friends were sitting, and Matt gave her a little wave and thumbs up. She waved back, then leaned in to hear the coach.

"If Paula gets the tip, we go right into the wheel," he said loudly in order to be heard above the growing din. The gym was nearly half full now, and a large group of parents and students from Custer had arrived and were making a lot of racket on the other side of the court. "If they get the tip, get right back in the zone. Jill, you and Lara have to look to cut off the pass, and forwards, you've got to help each other inside. Give them the long shots, but don't give up anything easy in the lane. Okay?"

They nodded.

"Then let's go!" They all stacked hands again and shouted "Let's go!" and then the referee was blowing his whistle to get things started.

Paula went high to control the tip, and Andrea set up near the free throw line as Jill brought the ball into the Custer court. The quick, rangy girl who had dazzled them with her warm-up moves jumped up to guard her and put her fingers in the middle of Andrea's back. Andrea twisted away to the left, then cut back, right at the same time that Paula made a similar move. Courtney went wide to the left to take Jill's pass, and then Lara rolled across the lane—the first one on the wheel. Andrea counted to one thousand two, then made her move across the lane.

Just as she started, she saw the Custer defender cut off by Paula, and almost simultaneously saw Courtney lob the ball toward her. She concentrated, caught the ball, wheeled

44

to the basket, and was amazed that no one was there to stop her. She put up a little jump shot from five feet and felt her heart move up to her throat as the ball bounded off the back of the rim, went high in the air, then dropped back through! The Scoopers were ahead, and she had broken the ice.

Her teammates raced over to pound her on the back. Too late, they heard Coach Forrest screaming at them to get back on defense. The Custer center, wasting no time, had taken the ball and fired a half-court pass to one of her guards. Before the Sturgis girls could recover, a second pass had reached the quick forward who had been guarding Andrea, and the girl had an easy lay-up to tie the score.

Forrest slapped his hands together in disgust, waited until the guards had brought the ball to half court, then called for a time-out.

"Now, listen," he said as they raced over and gathered around him. "You ran that play perfectly, but you can't stand around and pat yourselves on the back while they come right back on us and score. Understood?"

They nodded sheepishly.

"Okay. Get back out there and play heads-up basketball."

The first quarter passed quickly, and it became evident that it was going to be a defensive game. Andrea scored once more inside, Courtney had a long jump shot from the corner, and Lara broke down the lane on a lay-up.

Custer countered with two more baskets by its star forward, and a couple of free throws from the center.

The game stayed even early into the third quarter, when Forrest sent in Tracey for Courtney and Patty for Lara. The first time down the court, Jill looked past Tracey and threw the ball to Paula. But Paula held her position, tossed the ball out to Tracey, and watched as Tracey nailed a twelve-foot jumper.

Paula reached over and slapped hands with Tracey, and the girls dropped back to their defensive court. Seconds later, Andrea watched in amazement as Tracey seemed to come out of nowhere to pick off a Custer pass and then dribble the length of the court to score. Custer's guards moved cautiously upcourt on the next possession, and this time it was Patty's turn to make things happen.

With her ponytails flying, she suddenly leaped at the Custer guard with the ball, causing the girl to pull back and lose control. Patty dived at the loose ball and batted it toward Tracey, who picked it up and quickly passed to Paula. Paula took one step left, then put up a sweeping hook to score.

The Custer guard shook her head and called time as Paula gave Tracey a "high five" hand slap. Then both girls hugged Patty. Andrea grinned—Patty was hugging Tracey in return! She glanced into the crowd and saw her mother smiling and cheering, too.

Good old Mom, she thought. *Always seems to have the right answers.*

From that point on, the game was decided as Forrest rotated his players in and out and played cautiously. Trailing by six to eight points, the Wildcats were forced to foul, and Andrea and Paula each hit four free throws in the final minutes to seal the win.

As the fans counted down the final seconds, the team began celebrating and hugging each other. It was only an eight-point win, but for the long-suffering Scooper fans, the win might as well have been by fifty.

As the girls shook hands with the Custer players, Jill suddenly squared off against a Custer guard and gave her a shove. Everyone stopped in shock as Forrest and the Custer coach rushed over to pull the two players apart.

"What's the matter with you?" Forrest shouted.

"She was shoving me around the whole game," Jill said angrily. "I was just giving her a taste of her own medicine."

"She called me a name," the Custer player yelled.

"I called her a jerk. She's lucky I didn't hit her in the mouth," Jill responded.

"Get her in the locker room," Forrest said, directing his comment to the rest of the ream. "I'll go apologize."

Andrea and Paula grabbed Jill by the shoulders and pulled her toward the locker room. But Courtney smiled and said, "All right, Jill. Gotta stand up for your own rights, too."

"It was dumb," Tracey protested.

"That's for sure," Paula added her support. "All of us got pushed around out there, but it isn't worth starting a fight over."

They were sitting quietly in the locker room when Forrest came back in.

"All right. It's all smoothed over, but it was stupid. The next time anyone on this team pulls anything like that, she's suspended for the next game. Understood?" He looked directly at Jill, and she nodded.

"Okay, then let's forget it and start doing some cheering! We won!"

The girls broke into cheers as Forrest walked among them shaking their hands. Then he said, "See you in practice tomorrow," and left the room.

"Andrea, you were great," Paula said. "Everyone played great! And, Tracey, what super plays!"

Tracey blushed and smiled as several girls added their agreement.

"You did great yourself," Tracey answered, "especially the way you scored on that sky hook shot."

"Yeah, Paula, way to hit the sky hook," Lara said. She gave Paula a hand slap, then rubbed a hand on top of Tracey's head as she walked past. Tracey and Andrea exchanged grins. Andrea turned and looked over to Jill who was pulling on her jeans over her sweaty uniform.

With a scowl on her face, Jill reached for her blouse.

"Aren't you going to shower?" Andrea asked. "You'll get sick running out like that."

"So what?" Jill snapped. "Who are you, my mother or something?"

"Hey, hey—listen, I was just asking, that's all," Andrea said. She fought down a rising sense of anger. "Look, forget about the dumb Custer girl. Okay? The game's over." Andrea reached out a hand to show her goodwill, but Jill shoved it away, jumped up, and left. *So much for the sky hook, God,* thought Andrea, her cheeks burning. *And so much for you, Jill Bradford,* she was tempted to add. She forced the thought away.

She looked back at her teammates, but only Courtney was looking their way. Courtney smiled slightly but said nothing.

6
Tournament Plans

Jill missed school Friday. Andrea thought for a fleeting second about calling her at noon, and then decided not to. *She's just being a big baby,* she thought. *Let someone else worry about her for a while!* She dropped her thoughts as she heard a voice behind her.

"Hey, Andrea, great game last night." It was Matt and his friend James Bradigan. "I told you you'd do great on that team, didn't I?"

Andrea nodded.

"Tracey played good, too," Matt added. "You guys could have a pretty good team if you can keep Jill from getting kicked off it for fighting." He and James laughed, but Andrea frowned, and they both stopped.

"Listen, I didn't mean to get you upset," Matt began. "I was just, well, uh, forget it. It wasn't such a good joke, I guess."

Andrea shrugged, but the reminder hurt. "Forget it," she said. "I'm just—a little jumpy about her, I guess."

"Well—so's she," said Matt. "Jumps at anybody and anything. Ever since she hooked up with that Courtney. If you ask me, they're both nuts." He shook his head.

Then his look brightened up and he nodded to James, who gave him a little smile, turned, and walked off down the hall.

"Uh, Andrea. I was wondering if, uh, if you were possibly

thinking of going to the theater tomorrow night?"

"Sure."

"Well, um. Maybe afterward—I mean, maybe if there's enough time—"

"What, Matt?" Andrea said. "Time for what?"

"Well, for us to, uh, maybe stop off and get a Coke or something before you have to go back home."

Andrea suddenly felt warm inside, but she struggled to keep from blushing and gave him a smile in return. "Yes. I think that'd be terrific."

"Yeah? Well, great!" He shifted his feet uneasily, then grabbed his English book with both hands and waved it toward her. "Look, I gotta get to class. Okay? I'll see you tomorrow night for sure." He gave her a little grin and hurried away, just as Tracey walked up behind her.

"Where's he off to in such a hurry?"

"English class," Andrea replied, watching him go.

"English classes are over for today," Tracey said.

"Yeah, I know," Andrea said. Then she giggled, and Tracey joined in.

By practice time, Andrea was still in a good mood. She hardly noticed that Jill was still gone.

Forrest called the team together for a quick talk as soon as everyone was on the court.

"Where's Jill?" he asked.

"Sick," Courtney said. "I called her mom at noon."

The coach made a face. "Look, I don't know if she's sick or not, but everyone has to take full advantage of these practices. We're going to be playing two games a week from here on out all the way through November 6th, and we need everyone here as much as we can."

He paused and looked at his team before speaking again.

"And," he finally said, "I've got another little surprise for you. This year there could be a postseason tournament."

The girls broke into excited murmurs before Forrest held up his hands for quiet.

"I said *could* because everyone in the conference isn't going to get in. Only the top four teams, plus the four big junior highs in Rapid City will play."

"Yeah, but, Coach, we don't play all the conference teams the same, and we've got to play Rapid City North, too. That's not fair," Lara said.

"Well, fair or not, that's the way it is," he responded. "But we're off to a good start, because we already beat one of the teams figured to be near the top of the conference. All we have to do is win every game and we'll be in for sure."

The girls erupted in groans, and Forrest laughed.

"Well, listen. We'll worry about that later. Right now, we need to worry about Douglas, and I don't know a thing about them. I'm going to talk a little with Courtney about what kind of team they might have, and I want the rest of you to warm up on your own and get in some free throws."

Courtney looked pleased at the coach's comment. The rest of the team picked up the basketballs and started shooting. Andrea put up a long shot and watched it bounce off the rim. As she retrieved the ball, she saw Tracey whirl down the lane and toss up an underhand shot which rolled in.

"Nice shot!" she called as she dribbled up near Patty.

"Show-off shot, you mean," Patty said. "Sometimes I think I'm going to like Tracey, and the next thing you know she's showing off again. I just don't know about her."

Before Andrea could say anything in return, Forrest blew his whistle and called them all back in.

"Courtney says we can expect a rough game—even rougher than Custer."

The girls groaned again.

"I'm already one big black and blue mark," Lara said. "The only place on me that looks normal is the part covered by my brace."

"Well, even that may be black and blue by Tuesday night," smiled the coach. "We'll just have to hope the refs call a close game so we don't get beat up too much."

"Yeah, and if that doesn't work, just push 'em back," Courtney muttered. "I know I'm not going to stand around and get pounded on, that's for sure."

Everyone stared at her in silence. Courtney had spoken with the sound of hatred in her voice.

Andrea was not sure how to approach her mother about

Matt's invitation for a Coke. She decided to get dressed first, and then ask her mother if it was okay just before she left. She carefully selected a skirt and blouse, and put on a light eye shadow to accent her eyes.

Her mother called her to dinner, and she went despite the fact that she didn't feel a bit hungry.

"Going to the movie tonight?"

Andrea nodded and slid her peas into a neat stack on one corner of the plate. Then she cut several pieces off the pork chop her mother had prepared. She put a scoop of applesauce onto her plate and eyed it carefully.

"You feeling okay?"

"Sure. Just not too hungry, that's all."

"So, who you going to the movie with?"

"Probably Patty and Michelle. We'll probably see the others down there."

Her mother took a bite of her pork chop. "And afterwards? Got any plans?"

"Well, Mom, I was wondering if, uh, if—" she paused and gulped.

"Andrea. I have a good idea. Why don't you ask Matt if maybe he could go have a Coke with you after the movie. It might be a good chance for you two to get to know each other a little better."

Andrea nearly dropped her fork at her mother's remarks.

"Huh? Matt?" She blushed. "Mom. How did you know?"

"Mothers always know," she said teasingly. "Besides, I've never seen you wash your hair and put on that special skirt and blouse outfit to impress Michelle and Patty."

"And that's how you knew I wanted to have a Coke with Matt?"

"Sure. That, and the phone call I got from Matt asking if it would be okay."

Andrea laughed and walked around the table to give her mother a hug.

"You certainly are turning into quite a young lady," her mother said, holding her out at arm's length. "I love you, Andrea."

"I love you, too, Mom." Andrea hugged her again.

"Now get over there and eat your dinner. Matt or no Matt,

I didn't cook this for you to worry it to death with your fork."

The movie was great, and the Coke with Matt was fun and not at all embarrassing as Andrea first thought it might turn out to be. In fact, most of the other girls made a point of not going into the same cafe that Matt and Andrea chose.

They talked first about school, then about sports, finally about the other kids, both his friends and hers. He had just mentioned Jill and Courtney again when his mother walked in and signaled, pointing to the wall clock. It was nearly ten. Matt paid the bill and left a small tip, and Andrea felt like she was really on a date.

As they neared her house, he turned his hand toward her and she reached over and took it in hers. Then they were pulling into her driveway. She squeezed his hand softly, then took hers away as he opened the door and let her out.

"Thanks, Andrea. I had fun."

"Me, too," she said. "See you in Sunday school tomorrow." She leaned back into the car. "Good night, Mrs. Polovich. Thanks for the ride home."

They waited in the driveway until Andrea had gone into her house.

Her mother looked up expectantly. She was sitting on the living room sofa watching television. "Have a good time?"

"Yes. It was nice."

"And Matt?"

"I think so. He's a nice friend."

Her mother nodded pensively. "Yes, but like I said before, sometimes you have that look on your face that 'says he's a little more than just a 'nice friend.' "

Andrea gave her mother an indignant look. "Like what?"

"Like the one you had when you walked in the door." She chuckled. "Good night, Andrea. Sweet dreams."

"Oh, Mother." Andrea tried another indignant look. "Good night." She turned quickly so her mother couldn't see her big smile, and ran happily to her room.

In Sunday school Matt sat next to her, and Andrea was so pleased that she almost overlooked the fact that Jill was gone. It was only when Forrest asked her if she knew how Jill was feeling that Andrea broke out of her daydreaming.

"I don't know," she answered. "I didn't get a chance to call her yesterday." Suddenly, she felt very guilty. She knew it wasn't that she hadn't had a chance. She knew it was because she'd *decided* not to. Her face burned. She'd given up on her best friend. *Well, what did you expect me to do, God?* she fumed.

Coach Forrest's voice penetrated her thoughts.

"Well, if she doesn't show up for school tomorrow, I might give her mother a call myself," he said. "But I'd appreciate it if you'd check on her for me."

Andrea's face burned again. "Sure," she said unenthusiastically. "I'll call her today, after we get home from church."

Andrea left the classroom and found Matt waiting in the hall. For the first time since he'd started showing her some attention, she didn't want him there.

"Uh, look, I have to go right home. Okay?" She started to walk past him, and he held up a hand to stop her.

"Is something wrong?"

"No," she said sharply, "I just have to get going."

He pulled back his hand and stepped aside. "Sorry," he mumbled. "I was just going to ask if maybe you'd like to go bike riding, or something this afternoon."

She shook her head. "No. I've got to do some other things this afternoon. I—I'm behind on my studies," she lied.

Matt's face fell, and he turned away.

"Matt." She reached out and touched his arm, and he looked back with a confused expression on his face.

"Look, it's nothing with you. It's just me and something I've got to do."

"It's probably Jill again, right?" He had a bitter tone in his voice. "I don't know why you want to be her friend, anyway. She's just a troublemaker, you know."

"That's not true! She's just a little mixed up right now, and—and she needs a friend." Like I haven't been, Andrea added to herself.

Matt looked down at the floor and scuffed his shoe along the tile. His angry expression changed to sad.

"Sorry," Andrea said. She hurried away before he could say anything more.

"You look mad," her mother said as Andrea climbed into

the front seat next to her. "You have problems?"

"No. Well—yes, I guess," Andrea said as they drove out of the parking lot. "It's Jill. You know how she got into that fight with that girl from Custer?" Her mother nodded. "Well, then everyone got down on her after the game and she left the locker room mad. Then she didn't come to school Friday, and when Courtney called her mother, her mother said she was sick.

"I thought she was just mad yet, but now she didn't show up for Sunday school, either, so maybe she really was sick."

"And you're blaming yourself because you didn't go find out sooner? Is that it?"

"Sort of." Andrea paused.

"Andrea, you have a right to be happy for yourself, too, you know," her mother said. "You've been a good friend to Jill. You can't get down on yourself because you overlooked her for a couple of days."

"No, Mom, it's not that," she said. Her mother pulled the car over and stopped at the tone in her voice. Andrea glanced over at her, then began crying even harder. "I really did turn my back on her," she sobbed. "Deliberately."

Her mother reached over and pulled her toward her, and Andrea buried her head in her mother's shoulder.

"And it's not just Jill," Andrea sobbed. "It's Matt, too. I treated him bad back there in church, and now I've probably got him mad at me forever. I guess I was just thinking about how dumb I was with Jill, and then I acted just as dumb with Matt. What's wrong with me, anyway?"

"Sshhh," her mother said, stroking her hair. "There's nothing wrong with you. You're just growing up, that's all. Now, you dry your eyes and I'll drive over by Jill's house and let you off. You can talk with her for a few minutes while I go home and get us some lunch."

Andrea nodded, took out a handkerchief, and wiped her eyes and blew her nose. Jill's house was nearby, and they were there in a couple of minutes. "I'll be back in about half an hour to pick you up," her mother said as they pulled to a stop.

"Would you mind if we ate a little late and I walked home afterward?" Andrea asked as she opened the door.

Mom smiled. "No problem. See you about one, then."

Andrea walked slowly up to Jill's door, paused to compose herself, then rang the bell. Mrs. Bradford came to answer.

"Why, Andrea, hello. This is a nice surprise. We haven't seen too much of you the last few weeks."

"Hi, Mrs. B. I know I haven't been around much. With school and everything, seems like there isn't so much time." She forced a little smile and looked past Mrs. Bradford. "Is Jill here?"

"Yes. We were just getting ready to eat lunch. Would you like to join us?"

"No, thank you. I was just wondering how Jill was doing, so I asked Mom to drop me by on the way home from church. Would it be okay if I just said hello to her for a few minutes?"

"Of course. Come in."

"If it's okay, I'd like to just wait out here for a few minutes." She smiled again. "It's a nice day, and maybe Jill and I could just talk out here."

"Okay. I'll go get Jill. It'd do her good to get outside, anyway, after being cooped up in there for three days."

She turned and walked back inside, and Andrea went to the front step and sat down. She stared out at the lawn watching a squirrel busy hauling something from the yard into a nearby oak tree. The door creaked open behind her, and she turned to see Jill stepping outside.

"Hi." Jill's voice was lackluster.

"You feeling better now?"

"I guess. A little dizzy, though." Jill sat down beside her.

Andrea chuckled in spite of herself. "So, what else is new?"

Jill shoved her, but it was a friendly shove, and both girls laughed.

"Thought I'd better come over and find out if you died or something," Andrea said. "I don't think you've ever been sick three days before."

"I haven't," Jill answered. She extended both feet straight out as if stretching her legs, then pulled her knees back up to her chin. "I wasn't this time either."

Andrea glanced at Jill but said nothing.

"I needed some time to think about things."

"You okay now?" Andrea asked.

"Yeah, I guess. Things have kinda changed with us, haven't they?"

"Yeah, they have, but I'm still not sure why."

"Maybe because of Tracey," Jill said. "You two have gotten to be good friends, and I still can't stand her."

Andrea nodded. "And maybe because of Courtney, too," she said slowly. "I don't like her very much, but you two seem to get along great."

"We do," Jill answered. "But it's not the same as it was with you and me."

"Yeah, I know. I like Tracey, but I miss all the crazy things you and I used to do."

They sat quietly for a moment, each watching the squirrel again. Almost simultaneously, they looked at each other and started to speak. They both giggled and broke into a laugh.

"Let's be friends again. Okay?" Andrea said when they had stopped laughing.

Jill nodded, and they gave each other a hug.

"But I'm still keeping Courtney as a friend, too."

"I know. And one of these days I'm going to get you to like Tracey."

"Fat chance," Jill said. "But miracles do happen."

They stood up at the sound of Jill's mother calling her.

"I'll see you in school tomorrow. Okay?" Andrea said.

"Sure," Jill replied. "Must be a miracle. I feel better already." She reached out and gave Andrea a "high five" hand slap and then bounded back into her house.

Andrea walked down onto the lawn and paused to look back at Jill's house. It felt good to have her friend back, even on a shared basis. Now, she'd have to go work a miracle of her own to smooth things over with Matt.

"Thanks, Lord," she said aloud, pausing to look heavenward. "Thanks for helping me talk to Jill. Please help me with Matt, too." The squirrel chattered happily at her.

7
No More Hassles

Andrea looked for Matt at school the next morning, but didn't see him anywhere among the others. When she reached her locker, there was a note stuck in it just above the lock. It was from Matt.

"Andrea. We had to go to Nebraska. My grandma's sick. Talk to you later? Matt."

She folded it up tightly and slipped it into her book bag, wondering how it had gotten to her locker. Her question was answered a few minutes later when Tracey ran up beside her as she was walking toward her first class.

"You find the note from Matt?"

"Yes. But how did you—?"

"He gave it to his brother to give to John yesterday. John asked me to bring it in to you. I didn't read it."

"Thanks. Do you know anything more about their grandma?"

Tracey shook her head. "No, but I prayed for her last night at church. I'm sure everything will be fine."

"*You* prayed? I didn't know you even went to church," Andrea blurted.

"Sure I do," Tracey said, a little put out. "You ought to come and see it sometime. It's the country church out by Elm Springs. I live out there, you know."

"Yeah. Your folks have a ranch or something, don't they?"

Tracey shook her head. "No. I live with my aunt and uncle. My mom and dad are dead." She swallowed hard as she said it and smiled again. "Anyway, it's a real nice church. Hey, look, I gotta get to math class. See you at lunch, okay?"

She hurried off and Andrea watched her. She hadn't known about Tracey's mom and dad. She really didn't know that much about Tracey at all. The bell rang, and she had to run to get to English.

As the day wore on, she had trouble concentrating on any of her classes, and math seemed extra hard. She would have to get Tracey to help her review before the first big test.

Basketball practice turned out to be the best one yet as they got ready for the next day's game against Douglas. Jill was her old self again, and everyone worked hard at getting down a new play that Forrest was trying to teach them.

Back in the locker room, everyone was laughing and screaming and Jill started trying to snap Lara with her towel as they dressed.

"Girls, you better save up all the extra energy for tomorrow night," Courtney said. "Those Douglas girls are gonna be hittin' on you so much, you'll wish you had that towel on the court with you."

"Hah. Any of them try me, and I'll hit 'em back," Jill said.

"I hope so," Courtney answered. "I know I'm not takin' anything from them, that's for sure."

"You start hitting anyone and Coach will suspend you," Tracey said. "You heard what he said, didn't you?"

"Sure, but I'm not taking anything from them, that's for sure."

"That's your problem, Jill. You've got to quit trying to fight every time you don't like something." Tracey's eyes flashed as she spoke.

"Don't start telling me how to act!" Jill had raised her voice, and the rest of the girls stopped talking and looked toward her and Tracey.

"Okay. I was just trying to help," Tracey answered. Her voice was quiet, but it had an edge to it.

"I don't want any of *your* help." Jill whacked the towel down on the bench and continued getting dressed.

Andrea glanced from Jill to Tracey and back to Jill. Both

girls were mad, and she was mad at them for fighting with each other. Getting her new friend and her old friend to like each other was going to be about the hardest thing she would ever do. No doubt about that.

Andrea tossed and turned that night, dreaming first about Jill in a fight with some big, mean-looking girls in Douglas uniforms, and then dreaming about Jill and Tracey having fight. Worst of all, she dreamed about Matt fighting and that one woke her up.

By game time Tuesday, she was tired and crabby, and t bus ride to the air force base seemed to take forever, eve though it lasted just half an hour.

When they finished dressing and walked onto the floor, they were surprised to see the Patriot team warming up—not because they were there, but because they looked so normal.

"I thought you said they were big and rough," Andrea said as Courtney emerged from the locker room. "They don't look any bigger than us—maybe even smaller!"

"Well, once we start playing, you'll see," Courtney answered. "I'm tellin' you, you gotta be ready."

Ten minutes later, Andrea began to wonder if maybe Courtney wasn't crazy or something. Not only wasn't Douglas as rough as Custer, but the Patriots weren't even close to being as good with the basketball. By the end of the first quarter, Sturgis already had a ten-point lead. But Courtney was causing a lot of trouble.

"What are you trying to prove?" Paula asked Courtney as they came over to the bench between quarters. "You push and shove that center of theirs one more time, and I wouldn't blame her if she knocked your lights out. The only rough player out there is you."

"Yeah, well, she's got it coming!" Courtney said. "I thought you guys would be doing something to help me."

"Help you with what?" Lara said. "They aren't doing anything to us. If you want to get into a fight with them, do it when we're not around. Okay?"

Forrest signaled to Tracey to check in, and walked over to where the girls were talking.

"Courtney, you're out until you can get yourself cooled

off. I don't know what's going on here, but I'm not putting you back in."

Courtney glared at him and the rest of the team, then stomped over to the end of the bench to sit down.

Tracey started where she left off against Custer, stealing the ball once, scoring on a long shot from the side, and playing good defense. But twice when Jill had the chance to pass Tracey the ball for what would have been easy baskets, Jill passed off to someone else instead.

With two minutes left in the half, Douglas started to close the gap, and again Tracey broke free for a pass, but Jill refused to throw it to her. As she turned to pass the other direction, the Douglas guard stepped in, stole the pass, and drove the length of the floor to score.

By halftime, the Patriots were back within four points, and the crowd was yelling and screaming as the teams left the floor.

"Jill, you're out. Patty's starting the second half," Forrest said as he walked into the locker room. "I can't believe you didn't throw that last pass to Tracey."

"I didn't think I had a good chance to get it to her," Jill said. "Give me a break. I'm sorry."

Forrest shook his head. "Okay. Maybe. But Patty's still going in."

"What about me?" Courtney said.

The coach nodded slowly. "Okay. You're back in. You start for Andrea. No more hassles out there, right?"

She nodded.

"All right. Now, let's get out there and play like we did at the start of the game. If we do that, you'll win this one going away. And don't let the crowd get on you. They're fired up now, but if you play good defense and get a couple of baskets, they'll quiet back down."

Andrea slid in beside Jill on the bench and wiped a towel across her face and neck as the second half got under way. The Scoopers took the tip, and set up an offensive play.

"Get the ball to Courtney!" Jill yelled as Lara looked to pass.

Lara passed to Tracey instead, and Tracey dribbled right past her defensive player and scored.

60

"All right, all right!" Forrest yelled, clapping his hands. "That's the way to start. Now let's play defense!"

Sturgis dropped back into the zone, and as the Douglas center waved her hand for the ball, Courtney elbowed her in the side. She dropped the pass and Patty picked it up. Forrest muttered something under his breath, then turned to look at his bench.

"Andrea, get back in there for Courtney. Right now!"

Andrea went to the scorer's table to check in, and then sat down in front of the table to wait for a break in the action so she could go in. The wait wasn't long.

As Sturgis set up its offense, Courtney ran down the lane, took a pass from Patty, and scored. As she turned away from the basket, she gave the Douglas center a shove, and the girl toppled over on top of Tracey. Both girls went down in a heap, and the referee blew his whistle to stop play.

The Douglas girl jumped up and started toward Courtney, but Forrest got to Courtney first, grabbed her by the arm, and pointed toward the locker room door. Andrea started onto the court and then saw that Tracey was still lying on the floor. Tears were streaming down her face.

"I hurt my ankle," she sobbed.

The coach and the referee examined it, and Forrest shook his head. "It's not serious. I think you just twisted it. Maybe a small sprain. Let's get you over to the bench and put some ice on it for right now." He and Andrea helped Tracey to the bench and gave her an ice pack to put on the ankle. Then Forrest motioned to Michelle to check into the lineup.

Courtney disappeared into the locker room as Forrest looked over that direction. "Go in there and get her out," he said to Jill. "And tell her to sit on the bench and keep her mouth shut the rest of the game. If I hear one word, she'll be out the next game."

Jill hurried off to get her, and the game resumed.

From that point, it was close. Michelle was nervous, but Paula began to score from both inside and outside, including another hook shot. Late in the fourth quarter, she connected on four straight free throws, and Arnell came in to get two key rebounds and scored a basket herself on an off-balance shot that looked terrible but went in.

As the Scoopers lined up to shake hands with the Douglas girls, they had a six-point win, an injured player, and a problem by the name of Courtney. While the rest of the team shook hands, Courtney turned away, and stomped off to the locker room. The Douglas center paused to watch her go, but returned to shaking hands with the rest of the team.

There was no elation this time as they showered and dressed and got back onto the bus. They were 2-0, but definitely not a team.

The bus ride back was quiet. Courtney sat by herself, and so did Tracey, since she was using the entire seat to prop up her injured ankle. After a few miles, the coach talked quietly with Tracey for several minutes and took another look at the ankle.

Instead of returning to the front of the bus where he had been sitting, he stopped beside Courtney and sat down. Andrea could see him talking to her and saw Courtney nod several times. Soon, she could see it was Courtney who was doing all the talking as the coach listened.

Slowly, the rest of the girls started talking among themselves about school and some of their friends. No one mentioned the game. As they pulled into the school parking lot, the coach stood up and faced them.

"I want everyone into the locker room for a team meeting before anyone goes home. I know your parents are out here, but they're just going to have to wait for a few minutes."

The girls nodded and filed out. Andrea held back to help Tracey as she gingerly put some weight on the injured ankle.

"How's it feel?"

"Not too bad. I think Coach is right. It's probably just a bad twist or a bruise or something."

Andrea walked beside her as she limped into the gym. Forrest was holding the door for them, and his expression was serious. They entered the locker room.

"Okay, we won," he began. "And you girls who came in off the bench did a fine job. We could have fallen apart, but we didn't. That's the sign of a decent team." He paused and looked at Courtney. "The other sign of a decent team is one where everyone is up front with everyone else about why they're acting the way they do.

"I've had a talk with Courtney and I know her story now, and we could let it be at that. But she told me she wants to tell you, too, so that's another reason I had you come in here. I'm going to wait out in the gym. When you're done, you can leave, and I'll see you all tomorrow at practice."

He left the room, and all eyes turned toward Courtney.

She shuffled around to the corner of the bench where she had been standing and put her gym bag down in front of her.

"I, uh, I wanted to tell you why I got rough out there tonight, and why I was hoping you'd be doing the same. Okay?"

No one spoke, so she continued.

"That center—her name is Sheila. Sheila Conroy. She's one of the chaplain's daughters out there at Ellsworth. Anyway, me 'n her were friends over at another school we both went to in Nebraska. It was a school like Douglas at another big air force base. We always did lots of things together—goofin' off, you know, and things like that.

"One day, we were in the BX—uh, that's the Base Exchange, sorta like a big department store. Well, Sheila decided she wanted this little radio, but we didn't have enough money along. So, she just took it. When we were walking out, a guard stopped us. He found the radio, and then they took us up to the main office and called our dads."

She stopped and licked her lips and shuffled her feet again before going on.

"Well, we were waiting there and she started crying and saying what a disgrace it would be for the chaplain's daughter to get caught shoplifting. So I told her I would take the rap." Courtney shrugged her shoulders as the other girls gasped. "I told her old man and my dad that I took the radio, and that Sheila didn't do anything.

"After that, though, she spread it around how I nearly got her arrested. I couldn't believe it! And a lot of the other kids believed her, too. Some of 'em were on that team tonight, 'cause they moved over here about the same time Sheila and I did. They all treated me like dirt because of what she said. Real nice, huh? And she's supposed to be the religious one!"

Several of the girls murmured sympathetically, and Courtney seemed encouraged by their response.

"Even my dad believed her, even though I told him later that it wasn't my fault. So, when we moved here, he decided to keep me out of Douglas and move here instead. He said it was for some new influences, but really he just didn't want to have a daughter over there he was ashamed of. So, I was hot at those Douglas girls, and I decided to get back at them out there on the court."

She looked around at her teammates and shrugged again.

"Anyway, that's my story. I'm sorry I tried to get the team involved."

The girls began talking together and filed out of the locker room as Courtney picked up her bag and walked over to where Tracey had sat down.

"Look, Tracey, I didn't mean for you to get hurt. Okay?"

"Sure," Tracey said. "It's not feeling so bad now, anyhow. I'm sorry you had all that hassle with those girls, but that's in the past. There won't be any more hassles for you here."

"Yeah," Andrea added. "And you can't keep holding it against God because of one bad pastor's kid. Anyway, things are different here."

"Oh, Andrea, lay off," Jill said. "She doesn't want to hear your talk about why it's good to go to Sunday school and church. Okay? Come on, Courtney, let's go home."

Jill grabbed her gym bag and left, with Courtney trailing behind.

Tracey stood up.

"Jill just said one thing I agree with," she said. "It's time to go home."

Andrea laughed, and they left together.

On Wednesday, Matt still wasn't in school, but after basketball practice, Andrea was surprised to see him waiting at the church when she arrived for youth group. She sat down in the front row, and he sat behind her.

She turned and spoke over her shoulder. "I got your note. How's your grandma doing?"

"Better. Mom stayed down there, but Dad thought we should get back to school. We got back about four this afternoon."

Andrea nodded and fidgeted, not knowing what to say.

"Did I miss anything special in school?" Matt asked.

"Not really. Oh! Except in Thompson's class today, he said it was a really important lesson. I thought it was sort of dumb, but I wrote everything down that he said. If you want the notes, I can let you use them."

"Great! Do you have them with you?"

"Here?" She laughed and turned halfway around in her chair to look at him. "No. They're over at my house."

"Oh, sure," he said with a little grin. "Maybe I can get them from you tomorrow."

She nodded and turned back around. After a few seconds, she turned to face him again.

"If you've got time, you could come by tonight after youth group. Mom wouldn't mind taking you home afterward. Maybe we could have some ice cream or something, and I could tell you about some of the other classes you missed."

He smiled. "Okay, if it's okay with Dad. I'll go give him a call." He got up and started to walk away, then turned and came back. "You sure it'll be okay with your mom?"

Andrea stood up. "Maybe I better go call, too."

"Right," he said, and they laughed and started toward the office together.

"Math has been really bad this week," Andrea said. "But you do great in that, don't you?"

"Yeah, but I really need help in Thompson's class. I'm glad you took those notes because I'll need them. Hey, maybe I can help you with your math. If we have time."

"Sure," she said.

"How'd you guys do against Douglas yesterday?"

"We won. Paula played super. She had 16 points."

"Wow! How about you?"

"Ten." She held up both hands.

"All right!" He held out a hand for a high five. She slapped his palm and he caught her hand and held on. He looked into her eyes for a few seconds, then released her hand and let it fall.

Andrea looked at her hand, then slowly held it out to him again. He reached out and grasped it firmly in his own, and she smiled.

8
Tracey's Surprise

Thursday's game was against tiny St. Martin's Academy. This was one game the Scoopers expected to win. After warm-ups, they hurried back into the locker room for the pregame prayer and Coach Forrest's final few words. He startled them with his new lineup for the game.

"I'm putting Tracey and Patty in today in place of Courtney and Jill," he said. "If we're as good from the top of the lineup to the bottom as I think, then it shouldn't matter which five girls are on the floor. Besides, they've been playing good basketball in the games and in practice, and they deserve the chance to start."

Courtney sat looking at her shoes, her face expressionless, but Jill's face went from excited to angry.

"Okay, let's pray, and then go out and play hard."

The girls gathered around him, but Courtney stood back. Jill glanced at her, started to step out of the circle, then decided to remain. Forrest prayed, thanking God for giving the girls the ability to play, for the strength to have a good game, and for his protection from injuries to both teams. Then they clasped hands in the center of the circle, shouted "Let's go!" and headed back to the court.

"Good luck, Tracey," Andrea whispered as they came out of the locker room and started toward their side of the floor. "Hope you score twenty."

As the game got under way, Paula got the tip to Patty, but she immediately traveled with the ball. The referee signaled turnover, and St. Martin's went on the attack. The Ravens were smaller than the Sturgis girls, but quicker than Andrea and the others had expected.

A little dark-haired guard drove right past Patty, and when Andrea stepped across the lane to help play defense against her, the girl whipped a pass to Andrea's side and the forward there scored on a nice, soft jump shot.

"Sorry," Patty mumbled as Andrea ran by her, "my fault."

Andrea shrugged and set up for the offense. St. Martin's set up in a zone defense, and Lara brought up the ball and signaled a thirty-one offense against it. It was a special offense set for Paula to get the ball in the corner and then either shoot or pass inside to one of the forwards.

As Paula took the ball, the Raven defender jumped out to challenge her, and Paula lobbed the ball in to Tracey. Tracey found herself wide open, but instead of her usual nice shot, she shot the ball long and hard off the backboard. The ball came loose near the free throw line, and the St. Martin's guard picked it up, again drove past Patty, and this time went uncontested the length of the court to score.

Andrea shook her head in disbelief and glanced at the bench. Forrest, too, was shaking his head and leaning back in disgust.

As Patty and Lara reached half court with the ball, the St. Martin's guards leaped out to meet them and then surrounded Lara as she took a couple of dribbles and picked up the ball to pass.

"Tracey, Andrea! Help out!" the coach yelled as the girls stopped in surprise. Both forwards sprinted toward Lara, and she stepped ahead with her brace-side leg and forced the ball through the wall of arms in front of her.

Andrea beat the St. Martin's girl to the ball and saw she had Paula and Tracey two against one under the basket. She threw a quick pass to Paula and then watched as Paula tossed the ball over to Tracey as the Raven defensive player stayed on Paula's side.

"Finally," Andrea said to herself. "We can't miss this one."

But Tracey was unable to control the easy pass and covered her face with both hands as the ball skipped out-of-bounds and back to St. Martin's.

That set the tempo of the game for the Scoopers, and St. Martin's took quick advantage, streaking out to a ten-point lead by the end of the first quarter, and leading by sixteen points before halftime.

Forrest went back to his original starting lineup for the second half, but Courtney displayed a lackluster effort, and Jill was unable to get the rest of the team going, despite coming out with a lot of enthusiasm.

Even Paula was off the mark with her usually dependable inside shots, and by midway through the fourth quarter, all five starters were on the bench, and the other five girls were finishing up. Betsy, in as Paula's replacement, sparked a late rally by scoring two baskets and assisting on one more. But at game's end, the visiting Ravens had a 38-30 upset win.

"This was my fault," the coach said as he paced in front of the team in the locker room. "I didn't have you properly prepared for this game, and it showed. We're lucky it wasn't a conference game, and we have a couple of practices before Tuesday's game with Belle Fourche. We'll let this one be our bad game and move on up from here."

He left, and Tracey covered her face, then sighed and ran her hands through her hair. "I blew it," she said. "You can blame this one on me, not the coach."

"Oh, forget it," Andrea replied. "We lost and that's that. Now we have to do what he said and get ready for Belle."

"You must be dreaming," Jill said with a sarcastic laugh. "Nobody beats Belle, especially at their place."

"They're really tough," Paula agreed. "And they're big, too. They've got one girl who's about as big as a moose."

The others laughed.

"Sure, it's easy for you to laugh," she said. "But I've got to try to guard her. I saw her in camp this summer, and she's about six foot. Maybe even six one."

"Well, we'll just help you out," Andrea said. "If we help out on defense, I think we can win. Just because Belle *always* wins the conference doesn't mean they will this time around. Right?"

Most of her teammates only moaned in response.

By Tuesday, following the forty-minute bus ride to Belle Fourche, the team was scared. The coach had tried to get them to think positively about the game, but as each day passed, they seemed to be building up the Belle Fourche team more.

"There's no way we're going to win this game with this attitude," Andrea said to Jill as they finished lacing up their shoes. "Good grief, just because you guys lost to them last year doesn't mean they can't be beat this year. We've got a good team, too, you know."

"Andrea, they didn't just beat us last year. They cremated us!" Jill responded. "They didn't lose any games last year—didn't even have any that were close."

Andrea shook her head. "You're talking now like you were talking at the start of the year. You know we're a better team with a better coach. You know you're better."

Jill looked at her but said nothing.

"Well, don't you?"

"Yeah, I guess."

"Okay. Then let's go out there and play like we're a good team. I'll make a deal with you. You play hard and I'll play hard and we'll try to get the rest of the team fired up, too. At least then if we lose it won't be because we went out there and handed it to them on a silver platter."

"All right," Jill said. "I'll try."

Andrea slapped her on the shoulder. "Great. That sounds like my old friend Jill talking again."

Despite Andrea's and Jill's urging, the rest of the team played like they felt—scared. By halftime, Paula had not scored a single point, the big Belle Fourche center had 14 points, and the Broncettes led by 12.

Andrea and Jill both played well but couldn't seem to get the team to rally. Then with two minutes left in the third quarter, Forrest substituted Arnie for Lara and Betsy for Paula and took a time-out.

"Arnell, you know those long shots you like to take in practice?" he asked. Arnie nodded. "I keep yelling at you not to shoot them, but now I want you to shoot them. Okay?" Again she nodded, and an excited look came into her eyes.

"And, Betsy, Paula keeps complaining about being pushed around in there by that big moose. Maybe she's a moose, but I want you to go on a moose hunt." Betsy giggled and so did the other girls. "You start taking the ball inside on her, and maybe she'll foul. If she gets in foul trouble, the forwards are going to have to drop back inside to help her out, and that's when you start making good, straight passes back out to our forwards. Okay?" He directed the question not only to her, but also to Andrea and Courtney.

"Three or four baskets and we're right back into this ball game! Now let's go!"

The girls broke the huddle with enthusiasm, and Jill took the ball up court and right to the free throw line. When the Belle guards came to challenge, she pivoted away and tossed the ball to Arnie, who was set up between twenty-five and thirty feet from the basket. Arnie dribbled once and fired away, and a gasp came from the crowd.

The gasp turned to sounds of surprise as the ball arched through the hoop, rippling the net as it swished. The Sturgis bench erupted, and Arnie flashed a little grin and exchanged high fives with Jill.

Next time down the court, Arnie took the ball on the dribble and scored again, this time from even farther out. Again the crowd reacted with surprise, and the Belle coach signaled for a time-out. Sturgis was within eight.

"Okay," Forrest said as the girls gathered around him excitedly. "They'll be sending someone out on you now, Arnie, so I want you to get the ball in to Betsy, and we'll work inside for a couple of minutes. You get that big girl to foul you a couple of times, Betsy, and I guarantee you we'll have them running scared."

As Belle cautiously attacked Sturgis's defense, Jill stepped in the way of a pass and intercepted. Just as she had the first time, she took the ball deep and looked back for Arnie. As Forrest had said, Belle's defense was ready, and a guard came out to challenge.

Arnie started to set up for another shot, then rifled a pass to Betsy, who had trouble hanging on, finally controlled it, then pivoted and tried a shot. The Broncette center, caught off guard, swung wildly to try to block, got a hand on the ball as Betsy released it, and came crashing into the Sturgis girl.

The referee blew his whistle for a foul and watched as Betsy's shot, tipped by the Belle Fourche girl, caromed off the backboard, hit the rim, bounced around twice and dropped through. He signaled the shot good, and again the Sturgis bench was on its feet.

"Way to go, Betsy! Way to shoot!" Andrea exclaimed, hugging Betsy as she prepared to shoot a free throw.

"I would have missed by five feet if she hadn't touched ball," Betsy said under her breath.

Forrest's strategy worked perfectly, and the Belle cent went to the bench with her fourth foul early in the fourth quarter. Paula came back into the game and found the range, and Arnie scored on two more long bombs as time wound down. With less than one minute left, a twelve footer by Andrea brought the Scoopers to within one, but from there on Belle went to a control ball game and scored from the free throw line when Sturgis was forced to foul.

As the final buzzer sounded, the Scoopers had lost by three, but they left the floor cheering as if they had won. *Now maybe we're a team.* Andrea thought, as she "high fived" with Jill, Tracey, Paula, and even Courtney. *Watch out for us now.*

Buoyed by the Belle Fourche comeback, the Scoopers defeated their next two opponents, notching a fifteen-point win over Spearfish's Spartans on the Spearfish court, and earning a hard-fought 38-35 win over a previously unbeaten Deadwood team back on the Sturgis home court.

And by October eleventh, a Thursday, the team had its first real "blowout," dominating Newell, the smallest school in the conference. Playing them at Sturgis, the Scoopers won by nearly thirty points as all ten players scored.

"No one can beat this team now," Courtney said as they cheered and tossed each other in the shower afterward.

"No kidding," Patty shouted. "We're the greatest!"

"Come on, you guys," Tracey said. "We're not that good yet."

"Don't be such a downer, Tracey," Lara said. "We've got a 5-2 record now and we probably should have even beaten Belle. Look, we're 5-1 in the conference. We keep playing this good and we're in the tournament for sure!"

"Tracey's right," Andrea said. "We start acting cocky and some of these teams are going to shoot us down real quick." She got up and slowly crept up where Tracey was standing by the edge of the shower and shoved her—still dressed in her game uniform—into the shower. "But right now it sure feels great to be winning!" she screamed as Tracey yelled in surprise.

Andrea doubled over in laughter, then screamed again as Jill and Lara grabbed her from behind and carried her into the shower.

"We're number one!" she burbled as water cascaded down on her head and sopped her tennis shoes and uniform.

Practice was still lighthearted on Friday, and Andrea did start to seriously worry about the team's attitude. She didn't know that much about Hot Springs, but Monday's opponent was bound to be tough, especially after a bus ride of more than an hour and a half.

Coach Forrest finally stopped a lackluster scrimmage and had the girls run through some basic drills—almost like the opening week of practice. Then he blew his whistle and gathered the team around him to close the day.

"I'm concerned about your attitude," he said. "But, hopefully, we'll be ready to go on Monday. I've heard they have a pretty good center, and they lost to Deadwood at Deadwood. But don't go thinking you're a lot better than them just because you beat Deadwood and they didn't. We probably could have lost to Deadwood, too, you know."

Andrea eyed her teammates and could see they were not overly concerned.

Forrest laid down the basketball he was holding and took out some sheets of paper.

"This is a map to my house," he said. "I'd like you all to come over to my place for lunch Sunday afternoon. Do you think you all can make it?"

Arnie, Patty, and Michelle raised their hands.

"We've got a special missions conference at our church Sunday afternoon," Patty said. "It's supposed to go till about three, and all of us have to help. We're showing slides and having different exhibits of the way the people live."

"Well, then, let's have it about three thirty or four," he said. "In fact, why doesn't everyone try to go to their church for the missions conference and then all come over to my place? The conference sounds like fun."

"It is," Michelle said. "That'd be great if you could all come! We're raising money to send to our church's missionaries. So everyone come and give a lot of money! Okay?"

Everyone started laughing and talking at once, but Tracey slowly raised her hand, a troubled look on her face.

Forrest waved a hand for silence and pointed to Tracey.

"I don't know if I can make either one," she said. "I've, uh, got a couple of other things I might have to do."

"Oh, come on, Tracey," Jill said quickly. "Poor little John can get along without you for a couple hours a week, can't he?"

Tracey glared at Jill. "It's got nothing to do with John," she answered. "Even if it was, that wouldn't be a problem with something like this."

"Oh, sure," Jill said sarcastically. "John snaps his fingers and you jump. I've seen how you act with him."

"You don't know anything about how I *act* with him," Tracey said angrily. A tear welled up in the corner of her eye, and she brushed at it and started to turn away. "I have to leave," she said to Forrest as he took a step toward her. She started toward the locker room and Andrea ran to catch her.

Tracey had tears streaming down her face now.

"Tracey, don't pay any attention to Jill, what does she—"

"Leave me alone!" Tracey said. She stopped, keeping her back to Andrea and the team. "Just let me be. Okay? I can take care of myself."

Andrea nodded and backed away as Tracey continued on to the locker room. Seconds later she emerged carrying her gym bag and still dressed in her practice gear and ran from the gym. Andrea walked slowly back to the team.

"Man, what a baby," Jill said. "I thought she was supposed to be so grown up, but she can't take anything!" A couple of the girls laughed nervously.

"Shut up, Jill!" Andrea exclaimed. "Just let it drop."

Forrest cleared his throat and spoke again. "Just try to

make it over if you can. We'll start about four and go for an hour or so. And I'll be at your conference, too," he said to Michelle, "but I don't know about giving LOTS of money." He laughed, and the team members joined him, glad to forget about the incident with Tracey.

"Okay. That's it for today." He clapped his hands, and the girls headed for the showers.

"I suppose you're going to take Tracey's side again," Jill started as Andrea entered the locker room.

"I don't know," she answered. "I haven't heard what it is yet. But let's not start arguing, okay?"

She dressed in silence and was the last to leave, all the time wondering what it was that had made Tracey so angry and upset. By the time she walked home, she had made up her mind to call and get involved, whether Tracey liked it or not.

Despite that resolution, it took her half an hour after dinner and three trips to the phone before she got up the courage to dial. Tracey answered.

"I just called to make sure you were all right," Andrea said. "I'm not trying to interfere or anything, I was just worried. Okay?"

There was a long pause on the other end of the line before Tracey said softly, "Okay. Thanks."

"Sure. Any chance you can make the coach's party?"

"Maybe. It's a long way in from my aunt and uncle's place, and they have to haul me around enough the way it is."

On impulse, Andrea decided to extend an invitation.

"Why don't you come in and stay with me? You can go to Sunday school and church with me, then we can go to the conference, then over to the coach's place. You can stay over Sunday night if you want."

Again, there was a long pause on the other end of the line.

"I—I can't. There's something I absolutely have to do at my uncle's ranch, and I don't dare miss my own Sunday school class this week. We've got a special lesson planned out that we've been working on, and we'll be taking care of the main church service. I'm sorry."

"I didn't know you were in a Sunday school class."

"Sure, but it's probably not anything like yours. Like I told you before, I go to just a small country church, so all the junior high and high school kids are together. This Sunday we're going to do the whole church service for everyone, and we'll be practicing during Sunday school hour."

"Your Sunday school meets before church?"

"Yeah, usually. And the parents sit around and have coffee together while we're in class. Kind of a social gathering."

"Sounds kind of fun," Andrea said. "And a lot different from mine."

"You should come out sometime. I meant it when I said you have to come and visit," Tracey said, her voice brightening as she spoke.

"I will." Andrea stopped. "How about Sunday?"

"Huh?"

"Really! I'll come out there, and then Mom can bring us both back in later for the party, and you can stay over."

"Um, well, I don't know."

"Come on. Tracey, you've got to come to this party, and I'm going to get you there no matter what. If you're really going to be part of this team, you *can't* miss this party!"

"All right! All right!" Tracey laughed. "But you better know what you're getting yourself in for. Our Sunday school starts at quarter to ten, and that means you'll have to head out here by nine. No sleeping in."

"Great. I'll be there."

"You sure your mom's going to go along with this? That's two long trips for her."

"I'll talk her into it," Andrea said. "Besides, she keeps saying how she misses drives in the country. Now she'll have a chance for two."

"You're crazy, you know that?" Tracy laughed.

"Yeah, I know. See you Sunday."

She recradled the telephone receiver and let out a long sigh. Maybe she was crazy. She just hoped her mother would understand why she had decided to do what she did.

"Tracey, you're going to be part of this team and you're going to have a lot of friends because of it," she said aloud. That's why it was so important that no matter what, Tracey had to make an appearance at the team party.

9
More About John

Tracey's little wooden country church was beautiful in the October sunshine as Andrea's mother pulled into the gravel parking lot just after nine-thirty.

"Now, you're sure you know where her aunt and uncle live, right?" Andrea asked nervously, glancing at the church as she spoke.

"Andrea, you've asked me that a half dozen times," her mother replied. "Yes, yes, yes, and *yes*—and I'll be there by two o'clock. Now give me a hug and quit looking at the beautiful little church as if it were the county jail."

Andrea gulped, forced a laugh, and reached across to hug her mother good-bye. "Thanks Mom. I just know this is going to be right."

"So do I. Now get out there and be your usual sparkling self. Okay?"

Andrea smiled.

"Yes, like that," her mother said. "I don't like to brag, but my daughter has the prettiest smile in four states. Don't pick up any new boyfriends. Matt will be jealous."

"Oh, Mom!" Andrea hugged her again. "Thanks." She climbed out of the car as several other cars started pulling into the lot and stirring up a little dust.

"Andrea! Over here!"

Tracey gave her a warm smile and grabbed her by the arm.

"I didn't know for sure if you were really coming," she said, "but I guess I should've known. I thought I'd wait here by the door just in case. We have a few minutes yet before Sunday school begins."

They went through the door and down a narrow set of stairs into the church basement. The center part of the basement was set up with trays of cookies and several pots of coffee, and all along the outside edge were doorways leading into classrooms.

Tracey waved at several people and led Andrea past the tables and into a room on the far end. As they entered the room, Andrea was surprised at how bright and cheery it was, especially for being in a basement. Sunlight streamed through two windows which were about head high.

A middle-aged woman stepped forward to greet them, and Tracey introduced her as Mrs. Warner, her teacher.

"I'm so glad you could join us today, Andrea, but I'm afraid we won't be having a regular lesson," she said. "The youth are doing the morning worship, and we'll be going upstairs to practice."

"Thank you," Andrea replied. "I know about the service, but it'll be fun to watch. Your church is a lot different from mine."

"She goes to St. John's," Tracey said. "You've probably got more kids in your eighth-grade class than we have in my whole junior high and high school group together."

Andrea looked around the room and saw chairs set up for about fifteen.

"Uh, yeah, I think so. But yours looks real interesting, too," she added.

"Well, the kids certainly have a good time, and I think it's good that all ages get a chance to work on projects together," Mrs. Warner said. "I enjoy them all, too."

"This is how I first got to know John," Tracey said.

"I didn't know John went to your church," Andrea said.

"Sure. He's the only other kid out here who goes to Sturgis to school. He started giving me rides' into school once in a while last year, and we always got together for church activities and things. Next thing you know, we were just sort of going out together." Tracey smiled and gave a little shrug as she spoke. "I probably never would've even thought of him as a boyfriend. He's always so quiet."

"You mean there aren't any other kids from Sturgis here at all?" Andrea asked. "Where do they go to school?"

"All over. Lots of smaller towns around here. But we're all good friends and we do a lot of things together. They're all ranch kids like me, so we see each other at rodeos, horse shows, and things like that."

"You go to rodeos?" Andrea was amazed. "Do you have your own horse?"

"Yes. A little roan mare. Her name is Strawberry. I'll let you see her after church."

"Wow! If I'd have known that, I would've made friends with you a long time ago," Andrea said.

Tracey laughed. "Well, now that I know you better, I wish you would have." She motioned toward the door. "Oh, here's John. Come on, I'll introduce you."

Tracey gave him a little wave hello, and John waved back and smiled a smile that lit up his whole rugged face. "Hi," he said in a soft, deep voice. "You must be Andrea."

Andrea nodded nervously.

"Tracey's been telling me about you. Glad you could be here. Hopefully we're not going to make idiots out of ourselves up in church today." He grinned again.

"It'll probably be super," Andrea replied.

Most of the other kids had filtered into the room while they were talking, and Mrs. Warner clapped her hands and asked them all to sit down. She said a short prayer to open and looked up at Andrea.

"We've got a guest today from Sturgis. Her name is Andrea, and she is out here visiting Tracey." The other kids smiled in her direction, and Andrea smiled back.

"Well, normally we'd be getting into the lesson, but we've got to get upstairs and run through this church service. I hope you've all had time to learn your parts and get ready—especially you, John."

"Ready," he said. He leaned toward Andrea and Tracey. "As long as I don't faint or something," he whispered. Tracey slapped him on the arm, and Andrea chuckled.

"No wonder you like him so much," she said to Tracey as

they followed the group upstairs. "What's he doing in the service?"

"The sermon," she answered. "I can't believe he volunteered to do it. He's usually so shy. We'll have to turn the microphone up to full power so everyone can hear him." She giggled, and Andrea joined in.

Andrea sat in one of the front pews and watched as the rest of the kids walked through their parts, skipping the songs and John's sermon as they practiced.

Tracey slipped down beside her.

"Well, I suppose we're ready," she said. "I just hope John does all right."

"Were you, uh, well—" Andrea paused. "Were you already dating John when we first saw you with him last spring at school?"

"Good grief! No!" she said. "He was just giving me a ride to school once in a while, then. But I guess we went out a couple of times in the summer. My aunt thought it would be okay, because she and Uncle Ron both have known him for most of his life. And, I turned fourteen in May and Aunt Rita first started dating my uncle when she was fourteen.

"I don't know how many people know, but I'm really a year older than the other kids in my class. My mom held me back when I was in kindergarten because I had pneumonia and missed a lot of school."

The church bell started ringing, interrupting their conversation, and Andrea looked back as people started coming up from the basement and from outside and filling up the pews. The church held about 200 people, and within a few minutes it was nearly full. Tracey got to her feet.

"Gotta go get ready," she said. "If you want you can stay here, or you can go over and sit with my aunt and uncle." She pointed to where a youngish-looking man and woman were sitting with a small boy.

"I'll just stay here, if that's okay."

Tracey nodded. "Sure. No problem. Church probably won't go the full hour today with us in charge, but it should be different. Bye."

The bell rang again, and the pastor entered and welcomed the congregation and read the announcements.

"And now, I'm pleased to present Mrs. Warner's youth group for the Service of the Word," he said, and he stepped down and took a seat in the pew.

The service went quickly, just as Tracey had predicted. Her part was the reading of the first and second lessons, and then she returned to her chair. Another girl read the Gospel, and directed the congregation to the hymn of the day. As they finished the song, John made his way to the pulpit and stood, nervously waiting until the singing was completed. As the people sat down, he swallowed hard and began.

His voice was still quiet, but it was clear and crisp, and Andrea found herself caught up in the story of the Prodigal Son. As John told the story, he related things from the community and also brought out two magazine articles which tied into the text. Finally, he closed with a simple prayer, which he said with deep feeling, and sat down.

Andrea could hear a sigh ripple through the congregation at the conclusion. It was a feeling she shared. He had been excellent.

The service ended in three-quarters of an hour, and the youth group filed down the aisle and waited at the entrance to shake hands with their friends, parents, and neighbors.

Andrea held back until everyone else had gone through the line, and then congratulated each class member on a good job. Tracey and John were standing together at the end.

"That was just great," Andrea said.

"He was super!" Tracey exclaimed and gave John a hug. He grinned again and that infectious grin made Andrea want to hug him, too. Instead, she held out her hand to congratulate him.

"I really liked what you said," she told him. "I wish a couple of my other friends could have heard you."

"Thanks. I worked hard on it because I wanted Tracey to be proud of me. You know, I was thinking about quitting church and Sunday school and everything until I met her. Now, I'm really glad I stayed. She got me thinking about things—my life, you know, and what God could mean to me. Things like that. I realize I've got a lot to be thankful for."

"Tracey!" It was Tracey's aunt calling her.

"Excuse me a minute," Tracey said, letting go of John's arm and hurrying to where her aunt was standing.

"Well, you really did a good job," Andrea said, finding herself alone with him. "I'm glad I got to hear you."

"Like I said, I owe that to Tracey. I come from a poor family, and I used to think God gave me a raw deal. But Tracey helped me realize how much I really owe to him. My mechanical ability, my athletic skills. And even though my folks are poor, we've got a pretty good life out here on the ranch, and they've always given me a good place to live. Thanks to Trace, I started to realize how much I have because of him."

"I've got some friends who should talk to you," Andrea said, thinking about Courtney's comments about church, and about the way Jill turned God off and on to suit her own purposes. "You have a real faith in God."

"I guess. But Tracey's the real strong believer. You think about how she lost her parents and still has had the courage to keep trusting God. Now that's faith!"

Andrea looked over to where Tracey was talking with her aunt and uncle. She had really misjudged not only Tracey, but also John. She wished the others in her class could know about the real girl they had been condemning for the past year.

"How'd Tracey lose her parents?" Andrea asked on impulse.

"Car wreck. Over near Hereford," John said. "They were coming back from a rodeo at Wall and decided to take the back road. There was some construction going on, and it was near dusk. When they hit the loose gravel, I guess they lost control of the car and it rolled down into a ravine. They found them there the next day.

"It was just about two years ago that happened. Tracey was staying at her aunt and uncle's place, and she's been with them ever since. Her folks are buried in a little family cemetery they have over there."

Andrea hung her head slightly. Her own father had died when she was young, and she barely remembered the pain that had caused. To lose not only one parent, but both, when you were nearly a teenager must have been awful.

"Hey, you two, come on!" It was Tracey, walking toward them as she spoke. "Aunt Rita says dinner's at our place—for *you*, John."

He grinned again. "Thanks, but Mom's expecting me to be home today. Besides, you've got plenty to do with Andrea, and then you guys have that big bash back in town. I'll see you tomorrow. Okay?"

She reached out and took his hand and squeezed it hard before nodding in agreement. "Okay. Bye." She watched as he walked over to his car, got in and waved, then drove away. Andrea noticed that her eyes seemed strangely sad. Then suddenly, she turned back to Andrea.

"Come on. We'll head back to my place. We live just over that hill. About a mile and a half from here. Aunt Rita's a great cook. You're going to love dinner." She grabbed Andrea by the arm and pulled her over to where her family was standing, introducing her first to Rita, then to her uncle Ron, and finally to her eight-year-old cousin Jeff.

The dinner was, as promised, wonderful. Andrea felt totally stuffed by the time she forced down the final bite of a piece of apple pie for dessert. She and Tracey did the dishes, and Tracey motioned to the clock.

"Look, it's nearly one-thirty now, and your mom will be out by two-thirty or so. Why don't you walk around and look at things here. I've got to take care of a little project that I had set up before. You know, when I said I probably couldn't come."

"Okay." Andrea smiled a little, but she was puzzled. "Anything I can do?"

"No. It's just something I have to do on my own. If you don't mind, I'll have Jeffy show you the horses and give you a quick tour. Is that okay?"

Andrea shrugged. "Yeah, sure." She felt uneasy about Tracey's evasiveness, but decided there wasn't much else she could do.

Jeff came over then to lead Andrea out toward the barns. After a few moments, Andrea forgot about Tracey's behavior as he began talking about the animals and showing Andrea his prize calf, his horse, and Tracey's beautiful little horse, Strawberry.

The barn was quiet and the smell of fresh-cut hay filled the air as she stood patting the roan horse on the nose.

"Come on. I'll show you my fort," Jeff said excitedly, racing out of the barn and startling the animals. "Come on! It's just over here!"

Andrea laughed and followed him as he led her past the buildings and through a little meadow toward a small grove.

"I've got a tree fort," he said, "but I don't let Mom or Dad or Tracey come in. You can see it from the outside. Okay?" He looked at her for her agreement, and she answered yes. They reached the grove, and he raced to the base of a large cottonwood tree and pointed to a hollowed-out area dug beneath a large root. It was surrounded by several cottonwood seedlings which formed a little wall.

As she looked over the seedlings, Andrea saw Tracey. She was sitting down on the ground about a hundred yards away—out of the trees and inside a fenced-in area in another little meadow.

"Hey, there's Tracey!" Jeff exclaimed. "Let's go over by her." He grabbed Andrea's hand and pulled her out of the trees and toward the next little meadow. As they approached, Andrea could see Tracey was kneeling beside two grave markers inside the wire fence. She pulled back on Jeff's hand and signaled silence with her finger to her lips.

Tracey was crying softly and appeared unaware that they were nearby. Suddenly, she stood and looked upward.

"Lord," she said aloud. "Help me remember to live my life so that Mom and Dad would be proud of me. Help me to forgive those who don't understand me or who make me angry. And thank you, Lord, for the ones who are my friends. Especially, thank you for John. Let me do your will in all that I do."

She leaned over and pulled a weed from the corner of one headstone, turned around, and saw her cousin and Andrea standing there. She wiped at her eyes and walked out through the gate to where they were waiting.

"Tracey, I'm sorry. I didn't mean to—" Andrea said, blinking back the tears from her own eyes. "I didn't know what you were doing here. I—I'm sorry." Andrea bowed her head.

"Hey, it's okay," Tracey answered, reaching over and placing a hand on Andrea's shoulder. "You didn't know, and I should've told you." She pulled a handkerchief from her dress pocket and handed it to Andrea.

"I had to come here today. It was two years ago that Mom and Dad were killed, and I promised myself that I would always remember and visit their graves on that day." She reached out and gave Andrea a little hug. "I'm glad you're here to share it. You're a good friend."

Andrea gave a little smile and dabbed at her eyes.

"I wish I could be as strong as you are," she said. "And I heard your prayer. Your parents would be proud of the daughter you turned out to be. That's for sure."

It was nearly three-thirty when they got back to town, and as they drove past Patty's church, they were surprised to see the conference still going on.

"Hey, let us out here, Mom, and we'll walk over to the coach's house," Andrea said. "We can still get in on a little of the conference. Besides, Patty, Michelle, and Arnie will be here, and we can all go over to Coach's place together."

As they walked toward the corner of the church, they saw Arnell come around the far side of the building and take out a round can. She opened it and took out a wad of something black and put it into her mouth.

"What's she doing?" Andrea said, stopping to watch.

"Ugh. Chewing tobacco," Tracey said. "I'd know that can anywhere. I didn't know she was into that stuff. Yuck!"

The church door opened and the pastor and their junior high principal walked out together, deep in conversation. At the same time, Arnell moved along the wall on a path that would cause her to run directly into the two men as she turned the corner.

"Oh, no!" Tracey exclaimed. "If they catch her, she'll really be in trouble. We've got to stop her."

"How?"

"You run up and ask them how long till the conference gets over. I'll take care of Arnie."

She dashed away, her dress billowing, while Andrea tried to remain calm and approach the two men. She passed the

84

corner of the church and stopped them just a few feet away, as Tracey intercepted their teammate along the side wall. A few minutes later, Tracey and Arnell walked around the corner and joined Andrea.

"Hi, Mr. Filsman, Rev. Packard," Tracey said. Arnell just nodded.

"Tracey. Arnell," the principal nodded as he spoke. "Going into the conference?"

"Yeah. Arnie, uh, Arnell is going to show me where she's been working today. Coming, Andrea?"

"Sure. Excuse me." She nodded to the two men and hurried after the other two girls as they rushed right past them and through the doorway. "Hey, wait up!" she called, finally catching them at the bottom of the stairs leading into the hallway where the conference was being held. "What'd you do with that stuff?" She made a face as she said it.

"Here," Tracey said, opening her palm slightly to reveal the round can of chewing tobacco. "We started to go around back, but there was another group of teachers back there. Come on." She walked to the women's restroom, led the way inside, and dumped the can into the trash.

"You're crazy, Arnie. You know the school rule about that stuff. Besides, if you're going to play basketball, what're you doing chewing tobacco, for crying out loud. If the principal or those teachers had caught you, you'd have been kicked off the team—not to mention out of school for a couple of days."

Arnell shrugged but said nothing.

"You can chew that stuff if you want to," Tracey added, "but one of these days you're going to get caught. If you know what's good for you, give it up!"

She walked back to the restroom door. "Come on, Andrea, let's go over to Coach's house. I suddenly don't feel much like a conference." She glared at Arnie and walked out. Andrea just looked back at Arnell and then followed along.

They were halfway to the coach's house before Tracey said anything.

"I can't figure out why anyone would want to chew that stuff," she said. "Especially someone playing sports."

"Well, I don't know if you got her to think about it, but you certainly scared me," Andrea said.

Tracey laughed.

They walked another block and a car slowed beside them. It was Michelle's mother. Riding with her were Patty, Michelle, and Arnie.

"You girls like a ride?"

"Thanks," Tracey said, "but it's only a couple more blocks. I'd like to walk."

"Me, too," Andrea added.

The woman waved and started to drive on, then stopped again.

The car doors opened, and the three girls got out. They waved to the woman, and she drove away.

"Hi." It was Patty who spoke first as they walked up beside them. "We thought we'd walk along, if it's okay."

"Sure," Tracey said.

"Arnie told us what happened," Michelle said after they had walked another half a block. "If you two hadn't come along, Arnie would've been in a lot of trouble.".

"It was Tracey who helped," Andrea said. "I didn't even know what Arnie was doing."

"I am glad you came," Arnell said. "That you caught me—not someone else. I'll leave that stuff alone. Promise."

"Okay." Tracey smiled. "That's great."

"You guys get to the conference?" Patty asked. "I didn't see you."

"No, we were out at Tracey's place in the country," Andrea answered. "Hey, you should see her horse."

"You've got a horse?" Michelle said. "Wow! That's super! I wish I had a horse."

"Maybe you can come out and see mine sometime. I'll even let you ride her," Tracey replied with a smile.

"Really! And these guys, too?" She gestured at Patty and Arnell.

"Sure. Really."

They walked ahead of Andrea talking more about the horse and Tracey's ranch, and Andrea smiled to herself. It wasn't exactly like she had planned, but so far getting Tracey into the party was working out just fine.

10
Turning Point

The bus ride to Hot Springs was long, so the girls had come prepared with blankets, pillows, radios, and sack lunches.

The night before had been great—both at the coach's party and later at Andrea's house, where she and Tracey had talked long into the night about everything from school to boyfriends. The only problem with that was that now they were both tired.

"Math was awful," Andrea complained, closing her eyes and letting her head sink deeper into the pillow. The bus hit a pothole in the road and jolted her upright. Everyone in the bus shrieked.

"Math wasn't awful," Tracey answered from her seat in front of Andrea. "It was Thompson's class that was awful. I don't see how you get that stuff."

"I dunno, just do. But I'll never get math. Did you figure out those problems at the end of the chapter?"

"Sure. I got 'em done already."

"You've got to be kidding!" Andrea exclaimed. "Ouch!" The bus hit another hole and jolted her again. "Maybe you can explain it to me."

"Maybe," Tracey said, peering over the top of the seat back, "after you try it yourself first." She grinned.

"Big help you are."

They both looked up as Paula walked unsteadily forward

from three seats back and slid in next to Andrea.

"Hi," she said. "Mind if I join you two?"

"No. Great!" Andrea said.

"We were just talking about maybe having a Halloween party at Patty's house and inviting a lot of the kids from the class. What do you think?"

"Oh, wow! Really!"

"We were thinking that maybe if we all brought different things it wouldn't cost very much, and Patty thought then her mom would go along with it. If the weather's decent, we could be outside on their patio. Couldn't be any worse than being out at a football game."

"You're right about that," Tracey said, involuntarily shivering. "When is Halloween anyway?"

"That's the crummy part," Paula replied. "It's on a Wednesday, and everyone has youth group or something first. And then we have to convince our parents to let us stay out late, too. That's a bummer, for sure."

"I'll bet they'd let us stay till eleven or so, especially since it's Patty's place," Andrea said. "After all, we *are* eighth graders."

They laughed together.

"Hey, isn't that the weekend of teacher conferences?" Tracey sat straight up in her seat as she spoke. "There won't be any school the next day, because there's a teacher workshop on Thursday and Friday! I'm sure of it; I was talking with Mr. Roberts about it today!"

"Oh, wow! You're right!" Paula said. She squealed and jumped up and hurried back to where Patty and the others were sitting to relay the news to them. They all broke into wild cheering when she finished.

"Hey! What in the world is going on back here?"

It was Coach Forrest. He walked back from the seat near the front where he had been reading a sports magazine and grinned at his team members.

"We were just doing a little planning for a party at Halloween," Andrea said, "and we forgot about having some time off from school then, too."

"Oh? Really?" he said, sitting down across the aisle from Tracey. "How come?"

Paula wobbled back up the aisle to join them and sat down in the empty seat behind the coach. Both Andrea and Tracey slid closer to the aisle to continue the conversation.

"You may have school off, but we've still got two games that week," the coach said. "That's getting down to the end of our schedule, so they'll be important."

"Yeah, we know that," Paula said.

"Patty's maybe going to have a Halloween party at her place, so everyone was worried about being out too late on a school night," Andrea said. "But with no school the next day, I'm sure our parents won't mind."

Coach Forrest frowned, then brightened again. "So, tell me, how's school been going for all of you? No problems with anything, I hope?"

Soon, all three girls were talking and sharing not only stories about their classes, but also stories about friends and other things that had been happening in school. Arnell and Lara came up to join them, and they were all talking and laughing together when the bus slowed and turned into Fall River Canyon for the final five miles into Hot Springs.

"Wow, that went fast," Forrest said, checking his watch. He smiled. "Well, I'd better go work up some final words of inspiration for you guys. If we're going to keep this winning streak going, it's time to get serious."

He lurched forward as the bus picked up speed.

"Coach says they have a pretty good center—naturally," said Paula. "I wonder why all the teams we play have to have good centers? Sometime I'd like to play somebody two or three inches shorter instead of the other way around."

"Dream on," Lara scoffed. "Unless you're planning to take some growth pills real soon."

"We must have bad water, or something," Andrea added. "Seems like everywhere else in the conference the kids are so much bigger. Even in football. Matt says most of the teams they've been playing have a lot bigger kids."

"Yeah, but they don't have Matt," Paula said in a little singsong voice. "Good thing, huh, Andrea?"

Andrea turned red and kicked across the aisle at Paula, who artfully dodged the foot and laughed.

The bus jerked sharply as it hit another pothole, and

Paula fell forward, banging her right knee against the seat.

"Ow!" she exclaimed as the other girls laughed. Paula sat back and held the knee, tears welling up in her eyes. The laughter quickly subsided.

"Hey, you okay?" Tracey asked, leaning across the aisle.

Paula grimaced and shook her head. "I hit it right on the kneecap," she said. "That *really* hurt."

"I'm sorry," Andrea said. "I didn't mean to do anything to make you get hurt, you know."

"Not your fault," Paula said with a pained expression on her face. She slid her legs down into the aisle and stretched out the injured one. "Guess it'll be okay. Stupid bus!"

By the time they reached the auditorium, she was able to move the knee more, but in the locker room, the other girls could see a large bump forming on the left side of her kneecap.

"You better tell Coach about that," Arnell urged.

"No. I'll be okay. It hurts some, but I can move it all right. After we get warmed up I'm sure it'll be fine."

On the floor, it became apparent that Paula was favoring the leg, and to make matters worse it was easy to see that the Hot Springs center was more than just good.

"She's super, isn't she?" Jill asked as she joined Andrea in the lay-up shooting line. "I haven't seen anyone with moves like that since that girl from Custer."

Andrea nodded, bit her bottom lip, and glanced from the Hot Springs center toward Paula, whose own movements were being hampered by the knee.

"Someone better talk to the coach," she said.

She left the line and jogged over to where Forrest was talking casually to the Hot Springs coach.

"Paula's hurt her knee," she said.

Forrest turned toward the court. "Bad?" he asked.

"No, not real bad, but she's got a lump on it. She banged it up on the bus."

"Oh, great! Just what we needed. That girl for Hot Springs is pretty good." He nodded toward the Hot Springs girl as she drove under the basket and put the ball in on a nifty reverse lay-up.

"Yeah, that's for sure," Andrea said, feeling sick.

"But the rest of their team isn't nearly as good as ours. Look at them. That girl with the long, dark hair is pretty good, and that little girl with the blonde hair isn't bad, either. But, I think man for man," he paused, "I mean, girl for girl, we're a better team. We're just going to have to play a zone, and everyone else is going to have to help Paula stop their center."

He glanced up at the clock.

"Look, it's time to go into the locker room. I'll check her knee and we'll talk about it there."

Andrea ran back onto the court and signaled for the team to follow her in. There, the coach checked the knee, told the other girls what he had told Andrea, and asked them to stand for the prayer. As she had for the past five games, Courtney stood back away from the circle, refusing to clasp hands with the others.

The game became an intense defensive struggle from the outset with both teams in tight zone defenses and refusing to give each other any easy shots.

Courtney was having her best game so far, and both Andrea and Jill started trying to get her the ball. Paula was hurting, and twice during the first half, Forrest substituted for her.

None of the girls could stop the Hot Springs center, and even with the forwards and guards trying to help guard her, she still had eighteen points by halftime. Despite that, Sturgis had a 24-20 lead behind 12 points from Courtney and eight from Andrea.

"She's great. No doubt about it," Forrest said as the girls sat perspiring and sipping water on the locker room benches. "But I still think we're a better overall team. She's going to get her points, but if we keep the rest of them out of scoring range, we're going to win."

Through the third quarter, his strategy seemed to be working and Sturgis clung to its precarious four-point lead. With four minutes left in the game, two things happened that changed everything.

As the Hot Springs girl dribbled the ball downcourt and drove in for a hook shot, Paula tried to block the attempt. She leaped high and got a hand on the ball, and both girls crashed to the floor. The Hot Springs center got to her feet as the referee signaled jump ball. Paula remained on the floor, writhing in pain and holding her injured knee.

Forrest rushed out to where his center lay, and the Hot Springs girl knelt back down beside her as well.

"I fell right on the knee," she cried.

"I'm sorry," the other girl said. "That was a great block!"

Paula tried to smile through her tears. "Thanks," she said. "You didn't do anything to me. I just fell on it."

Forrest helped her to her feet, and Courtney and Andrea supported her and got her over to the bench.

Betsy checked back in, lost the jump ball, and watched as the dark-haired Hot Springs forward took the tip and scored. It was only the second basket by anyone other than the center.

On the next play, Lara brought the ball into the free throw lane, found herself surrounded, and flipped a pass back to Patty. The Hot Springs center seemed to come out of nowhere, intercepted the pass, and dribbled the length of the court to score.

Suddenly, the game was tied, and that was how the fourth quarter ended—tied at 37.

Early in the overtime, Jill drew her fifth foul trying to slap the ball away from the center. Then Courtney fouled out just fifteen seconds later, also trying to help against the center. Both times, the Hot Springs girl scored from the free throw line and the Lady Bison were in control.

With three starters on the bench, the Sturgis team could not get back on track. The game ended 45-41. The Hot Springs center had scored 37 points.

The drive home seemed like an eternity. As the bus passed Rapid City and started up the freeway towards Sturgis, Coach Forrest walked down the aisle and stood supporting himself between two seats. The bus driver turned on the interior lights, and the girls sat up in their seats to face the coach. Andrea had been crying, and she could see that many of the others had, too.

Forrest cleared his throat. "Who thinks it was her fault that we lost this game tonight?" he asked.

Andrea raised her hand.

"Why you?"

"I'm the one who made Paula hurt her knee. If we wouldn't have been goofing off, it wouldn't have happened."

The coach turned to Paula.

"Do you blame Andrea for what happened to your knee?"

Paula shook her head.

"Okay. Who else?"

Patty raised her hand. "I, uh, I played really rotten, and I didn't help much stopping that girl—especially in the overtime." She looked around at the other girls. "I'm sorry I let you all down."

They started to murmur different things in response, and Forrest cut them off.

"Hold it! How many others are going to hold up a hand and tell me they did something that cost us the game?"

Slowly, each one of the girls raised her hand.

Forrest smiled. "Girls, I've got news for you. Not one of you cost us this game tonight, and neither did I. You girls went out there and played your hearts out, and you lost. That's part of life. Sometimes you lose the ones where you give it all you have. Sure, you made some mistakes out there, but everyone makes mistakes once in a while.

"The important thing is that we learn from our mistakes and learn from an experience like this loss. The way that center from Hot Springs was playing tonight, I don't think King Kong could've stopped her."

That drew laughter from the team, and Andrea could feel a bit of the tension disappear.

"You know, we went into that game tonight with big heads." They started to protest, but he shook his head and waved a hand to stop them.

"Yes, we did, and you know it. We'd been winning, and we were getting cocky. Even I was beginning to think we were going to keep winning easily, and we just weren't prepared for tonight. I said this before the game, and I'll say it now. We are a better *team* than Hot Springs. I think we could beat them most of the time. Tonight, they had a great individual effort, and they won."

He stopped and appeared to be choosing his next words. Andrea watched him carefully, wondering what it was he wanted to say.

"I think we can grow from this loss. Girls, I'm asking you not to blame anyone for the loss—especially yourselves. It's from here on out that you find out what you are made of. Playing on a winning team is easy. It's easy to go into the locker room after a win and congratulate each other and be proud."

He lowered his voice slightly. "Going into the locker room and telling your teammate that she did a good job, even when you lost, is hard. But remember this, being proud of your efforts and your teammates when you lose is even more important than doing so when you win. I want you to hold your heads up, because I think you have a right to be proud.

"I know I'm proud to be coaching a team that played as hard as you did out there tonight." He gave them a big smile. "Now, let's start thinking about how we're going to defeat Douglas Thursday night!"

The girls broke into loud cheers as the bus left the freeway and headed into Sturgis. Andrea actually felt as though they were returning from a win.

As they clambered out of the bus, all the players shook the coach's hand.

"You know, you had eighteen points tonight," Forrest said to Andrea when it was her turn to grasp his hand. "You thought you let the team down. I think you kept us in the game. Keep up the good work."

Andrea skipped down the bus steps, said good night to her teammates and hurried to the car where her mother was waiting.

"Hi," she said cheerfully. "Great night, isn't it?"

"You certainly are happy," her mother responded. "Must've been another big win for the Scoopers, huh?"

"Nope. We lost. But we played great, anyway. We'll get 'em next time. Anything to eat at home? I'm starved!"

"Sure!" Her mother laughed. "You may have lost the game, but your attitude sure does beat all!"

11
Comeback Trail

"Belle Fourche is still unbeaten, but we're right in the battle for one of those other three tournament spots despite our loss," Coach Forrest began as they opened practice Tuesday. "Paula's going to take some time off from hard workouts today and tomorrow, but she'll be practicing on her free throw shooting, and I still plan to play her Thursday. The rest of you need to work on polishing your game skills. Okay?"

Practice went extremely well, and Andrea could feel the team's enthusiasm. They were out to prove that they belonged near the top of the conference and that the loss wasn't going to keep them down.

Andrea felt good when she came out of the gym, and she felt even better when she saw Matt and a couple of his friends walking toward her from the football field. Matt waved good-bye to the other two boys, and they turned up the street.

"Hello. I was hoping you'd be walking home tonight."

"Hi," she answered. "Guess I'm going to be doing that about every night unless it starts to get too cold or rainy or something. You have football?"

"Yeah, but we finished early. We're going to scrimmage Newcastle tomorrow over at their place, so Coach Pierce thought we should get home and get our homework all caught up. We probably won't get back until youth group starts, and some of the guys have tests on Thursday."

"We play again Thursday," Andrea said. "Here. Think you can come?"

"Sure. I've been wanting to see you play again," said Matt. "Heard you scored eighteen points last night. That's super!"

They were nearing the street corner where Matt would turn off toward his house. Matt stopped.

"Andrea, would it be okay if I walked you the rest of the way home? I don't mind having to walk back after."

"Really? You sure?"

"Yeah."

"Okay." She smiled, and they started walking again.

"We play a home football game Saturday, and I was hoping you would be there," he said. "It'll be our third game, you know, but the first one here. We're playing at one thirty."

"I know that," she smiled. "I haven't been living on Mars, or someplace else, you know."

"Sure. I just wanted you to know that I was hoping you'd come. And afterward, my mom is going to have a little barbecue over in the park by Jill's place. I, uh—" he paused. "I was wondering if maybe you could come to that, too."

He stopped, waiting expectantly for her answer. Andrea stared at him in the growing dusk. A car with some high school kids in it whizzed by.

"Hi, lovebirds!" someone shouted from the window. Raucous laughter followed as the car zipped away.

Matt blushed. "Sorry about that. Probably some friends of my brother's. You probably won't want to be seen walking with me now."

"No! I mean, no, that's not true. I *like* being seen with you. I'm glad you like me."

Matt grinned, a great big ear-to-ear grin. "Well, come on." He turned to continue walking.

"I'll be there Saturday."

"Huh?" He stopped again.

"Saturday," she smiled. "I'll come to your barbecue."

"Really?"

She nodded enthusiastically. "Sounds fun."

"It will be," he said, stepping closer. "I'm glad you can come."

"Me, too." She reached out and took his hand and they walked on, not saying anything further. At her driveway, Matt sighed.

"Well," he said. "I'll see you in school tomorrow. Maybe we can walk home together again another night when practices are over at the same time?"

She nodded.

Matt released her hand and started to turn away.

"Matt." He stopped at the sound of her voice. "Thanks again." She leaned forward and kissed him gently on the cheek, then turned and hurried up the driveway. "See you tomorrow!" she shouted as she reached the door. She turned and waved. He waved back and sprinted away, wildly swinging his gym bag as he ran.

Andrea laughed. This was turning into the best school year ever, and it still wasn't even two months old.

The Douglas game on Thursday went a lot like the game against Douglas had earlier, only this time Courtney was a model player and Jill was the one causing all the trouble. Jill was especially insistent on playing rough against the girl who had been Courtney's problem from before.

By halftime Jill's play was taking its toll. Not only had she angered the Douglas girls, but she also had been whistled for her fourth foul.

"Jill, what are you trying to prove?" Andrea whispered angrily as they walked back into the locker room. "You're going to foul out if you keep this up."

"So what? Somebody's got to stick up for Courtney, and we already know what the coach would do to her if she tried anything. I'm just showing her she's got a friend. Okay?"

"Suit yourself," Andrea answered. "But don't sit around on the bench feeling sorry for yourself after you get that next foul."

Coach Forrest walked in, looking angry.

"We're not changing anything the second half," he said. "I want you to go out and keep working on our offense and really play this two-one-two zone tough. If they can't score, they can't beat us." He turned and drew a couple of diagrams on the blackboard and explained them.

"Okay. Patty, you're starting the second half for Jill, and, Arnell, you can plan to play quite a bit this half, too. Jill, you're out for the rest of the game."

Her face fell in disbelief.

"But I've only got four fouls," she began.

"That's four too many from what I've been seeing."

The team ran back onto the floor to the cheers of the crowd, and Andrea waved to her mother, then located Matt and waved to him, too. She had been hoping to have a good game with both of them here cheering, but so far it was Lara who was setting the pace. The little guard had scored three baskets and made great passes for a half dozen more.

Maybe this half, she thought. But the second half saw no improvement in her game.

Instead, Paula began to regain her confidence as her injured knee held up well, and Patty turned the second-half starting opportunity into a chance to have her best game.

With Paula shooting well inside and scoring from the free throw line and Patty setting up the plays, the Scoopers won by ten points over the much-improved Douglas squad.

Jill looked downcast as she left the floor, and Andrea watched as Courtney ran over and draped an arm around the feisty guard's shoulders and walked with her to the locker room.

"That was crummy," Tracey said. "Courtney probably put Jill up to that, and then Jill gets all the heat. Now she's over there playing big sister and showing Jill how much she cares. Some friend."

The problem was, Andrea thought, Jill undoubtedly *was* believing that Courtney was a good friend for consoling her. *I wish I could get Jill to realize how Courtney is using her*, thought Andrea. *But how—without making it sound like a bunch of sour grapes?*

Twice on Friday Andrea tried to make small talk with Jill, but each time someone else interrupted and they never did get into the matter about Courtney. At basketball practice, Jill was gone.

Andrea went to the high school football game that night

and sat with a lot of other eighth graders in one section. Below her, she saw Jill and Courtney come in laughing and talking with two sophomore boys.

"Hey, how come Jill's here and she missed practice?" Lara asked, leaning in over Andrea's shoulder. "She's going to be in big trouble for that."

"I don't know, but I'm sure she's got a good excuse," Andrea half shouted as the crowd noise increased. "You know Jill!"

She kept an eye out for Jill and Courtney the rest of the game, but didn't see them again. Jill seemed to be begging for trouble, and at the rate she was going, she was going to get a double dose.

Saturday came, and with it, a perfect day for the junior high football game. Andrea was so intent on watching Matt play, she didn't even see her old friend approach.

"You coming to Sunday school tomorrow?" Jill asked the question matter-of-factly as she dropped into a seat next to Andrea and chomped down hard on a hot dog she was carrying.

"Huh?" Andrea jumped at the sound of Jill's voice.

"Sunday school," Jill said. Her words were muffled as she chewed a big mouthful of hot dog.

"What are you doing here?" she asked Jill as her friend took another big bite, then yelled something unintelligible toward the field. She finished chewing and swallowed.

"Watchin' the game. What else? Isn't that why you're here?"

"Well, sure, but I didn't expect you, that's all."

"I see we're winning," Jill responded. "Matt playing good?"

"Sort of. He scored one touchdown, but last time out he fumbled, and that's how Spearfish scored." Andrea glanced back at the field and joined in the cheering as Matt and another Sturgis player tackled the Spearfish quarterback.

"What do you mean am I coming to Sunday school?"

"It's not a trick question," Jill said in disgust.

"All right. Of course I am. Why?"

"Because, I just thought we might sit together or

something." She paused and finished off the hot dog. "I mean, if I go."

Andrea looked back at the football field. After a couple minutes, she spoke again.

"Maybe you ought to bring Courtney along sometime. She might like it."

Jill snorted. "Hah! That'd be the day!" She snickered. "But I'll ask her sometime and see what she says—just for a good laugh."

The crowd roared, and both girls turned their attention back to the field. Andrea leaped to her feet and joined in the cheering. Matt had the ball and had broken clear on the far side of the field. Now, it was between him and one Spearfish defender to see whether or not he would score.

At the Spearfish twenty-five yard line, Matt suddenly pulled up, letting the Spearfish player race right by him. He cut back toward the center of the field and went down hard as another defensive player caught up and made the tackle. Matt's sideline move had worked against him.

The crowd let out a loud groan as Matt fell, and Andrea held her hands to her face. The defensive player jumped up, but Matt remained down. The Sturgis coach ran onto the field as the referee signaled an injury time-out. For several long moments the coach knelt beside Matt; then Matt got slowly to his feet and wobbled off the field.

The crowd cheered, and Andrea sank back onto the bleacher seat.

"Don't worry, he'll be okay," Jill said, sitting beside her. "Game's almost over anyway." She eyed Andrea. "You really like him, don't you?"

"I guess so."

"I do, too. But I don't have a chance with him. Good thing Courtney's moved here. She's helped me get to know a lot of other boys. Older boys, you know?" Her voice had a sound of superiority. "Well, I gotta get going," Jill added. "Maybe I'll see you tomorrow in church."

Andrea reached out and grabbed her by the arm.

"Hey, how come you missed practice yesterday? I saw you at the game last night, so I know you weren't sick."

"I dunno. Guess I just didn't feel like coming. Besides,

Forrest is mad at me anyway, so I won't get to start next game. Might as well take it easy a time or two."

"You'll get yourself benched for sure if you keep that attitude."

Jill shrugged. "Maybe. Maybe not." The crowd cheered again, and they looked at the field. The game was over, and Sturgis had won.

"I'll see you later. You better go see how Matt's doing." She turned and walked away.

Matt had been shaken up but not badly hurt on the tackle, and now he was cheering with his teammates as they came off the field.

"See you at the park!" he shouted. "Mom and Dad will be over there soon, so just go on over! Okay?"

Andrea waved in response. She walked to the main gate and turned toward the direction of the park. She had gone about half a block when a car slowed beside her and honked.

"Andrea! Where you headed?"

It was Tracey and John in John's car.

"Over to the park. I'm going to a barbecue."

"Polovich's?" Tracey asked.

"Uh-huh. But how did you—?"

"So are we." Tracey swung open the door. "Come on. Hop in. You can ride over with us."

Andrea climbed in on the passenger side and smiled at John.

"Matt's brother asked John and me to come to this, too," Tracey said. "Then we're going with him and his girl friend to a movie. Hey, you and Matt oughta come, too."

Andrea blushed and shook her head. "No. Not tonight. I went to the football game last night, and I told Mom I'd stay home. Besides, we're not really dating or anything. We're just good friends."

"Okay," Tracey said. "But sometime, you and Matt and John and I are going to go do something together." John nodded in agreement.

"Well, we are now," Andrea grinned. "We're going to a barbecue together."

"That's true," John said in his rich voice, "and if I don't get moving, we're going to miss out on all the food. You don't know yet about Matt's brother." They all laughed as he shifted into gear and pulled away.

The Scoopers' game Monday was a rematch with Newell. Before long, it became a ragged contest with both teams doing a lot of fouling. Jill didn't give Forrest the chance to not start her in the game. She wasn't there at all.

Newell was no match for the Scoopers, and the game went to Sturgis.

The next day, Jill was back on the practice court as if nothing had happened, and Forrest seemed to make a point of saying nothing to her about her absence.

At game time Thursday, the largest crowd of the year was on hand. Belle Fourche had been kicking Sturgis girls' teams around for years, and for the first time, it looked like one of the Sturgis teams had a chance to challenge them.

"If we constantly help out on defense, we can stop their center and we can win this game," Forrest said as he wrapped up his pregame talk. "Now, everyone has to hustle all the time. If you don't, we won't have a chance."

"Coach, will I be starting?" It was Jill.

"No. I'm starting Lara and Patty."

Jill's face darkened. "Well, that's okay," she responded. "I'm not feeling very good, anyway. I don't think I can play."

The coach's face remained unchanged. "Okay. I'm glad you told me." He turned and pointed to Tracey. "Tracey, I'm going to be playing you some at guard tonight. Think you can handle it?"

The room grew silent. Finally, Tracey nodded. "I'll do the best I can. I've never played it before."

"I know that. Okay, let's head out and give them a game they won't forget." He held his hand out, and they crowded around him, clasped hands, and yelled "Let's win!" The team ran onto the floor to a roar from the excited crowd.

Unlike the first Belle Fourche game, Sturgis opened this time as if they were the favorites instead of the other way around, and the crowd got behind them with their cheers.

The score was tied at halftime, and still tied at the end of the third quarter. Paula scored fifteen points, but went to the bench early in the fourth quarter with her fifth foul.

"Betsy has to keep up the defensive pressure on their big girl and everyone—and I mean *everyone*—has to help her," Forrest said sharply as they took a time-out. "Andrea, I want you to start taking some shots along the side. Guards, come out and try to get some steals at half court if you can."

The girls broke the huddle, and on the next possession, Andrea took a pass from Tracey, dribbled to the corner, and took a shot. It rattled in the rim and fell through. Twice more she connected from near the same spot, but each time the Belle Fourche center countered with shots inside.

With thirty seconds left, Andrea missed on a fifteen-foot shot from the side, and Belle Fourche controlled and called time-out. The score was tied at thirty. "Just play the ball and play your best defense!" Forrest shouted to be heard above the crowd noise.

Andrea gulped some water from a bottle, slapped her teammates on their backs, and held her hands into the center of the huddle. "Come on, girls!" she urged. "Don't give it away! Let's win!"

"Let's go!" they all yelled, breaking the huddle and setting up in their defense.

They watched as Belle's girls patiently passed the ball. With ten seconds left, the right-side guard took two dribbles in Andrea's direction, then lobbed the ball toward the forward on that side. Andrea leaped for the pass, missed it, and watched in agony as the girl turned to shoot.

Out of nowhere, Tracey appeared to challenge, and the girl, startled, tried to release the shot. The ball slipped, and Tracey grabbed it with both hands.

Andrea scrambled to her feet and started upcourt, and Tracey winged the ball toward her. The pass was perfect, and Andrea scored on a breakaway lay-up with two seconds left. The Scoopers had an upset 32-30 win.

The locker room was pandemonium as everyone first hugged Tracey, then Andrea, then Tracey again. Only Jill sat silently on the bench in front of the locker, a scowl on her face as she slowly dressed.

12
Curfew

"Tracey! What are you doing here?"

Andrea jumped up from the pew in which she was sitting as Tracey and John walked in and sat down in front of her.

Tracey grinned. "We just thought maybe we'd better check this place out," she said. "After all the bragging you do about your church, we thought it must be worth a visit."

"Well, at least you could warn a person," Andrea said. "I about passed out just now."

Tracey glanced over Andrea's shoulder. "If you about passed out when you saw me, you better sit down before you look at who's coming in the door right now."

Andrea turned slowly and looked. It was Jill. And beside her stood Courtney.

"I don't believe it!" she whispered.

The two girls gestured toward one of the back rows and sat down. Andrea waited until they were looking forward and waved. Jill returned the wave, but Courtney stared straight ahead, unmoving.

"I just don't believe it!" Andrea said again, slowly sitting.

John burst into laughter. "I wish I had a camera now," he said. "You have the weirdest look on your face."

Andrea barely heard the sermon. All through it, she resisted a tremendous urge to turn around and see if the two girls were still in the church. When the final blessing was said, she jerked her head around and saw them standing and talking to an older couple sitting beside them.

"So, where's this Sunday school class of yours?" Tracey asked.

"Um, in the Fellowship Hall, over on the west side," Andrea said hurriedly. She saw Jill and Courtney start to make their way out of the pew. "Tracey, do you mind if I run back there and talk to them a minute? I'll meet you in the hallway by the main door. Okay?"

Tracey nodded, and Andrea scrambled out of the pew and excused herself through the crowds of people filling the aisle. By the time she reached the doorway, Jill and Courtney were nowhere in sight.

"You lose somebody?"

It was Coach Forrest. He was smiling as he approached her.

"I was hoping to find Jill and Courtney. They were sitting in the back, but I couldn't get down the aisle fast enough," Andrea gasped. "You didn't see them, did you?"

He shook his head. "Nope, but I'm sorry I missed them. I'm surprised Courtney was even here. I thought she was antichurch."

"She is—or was," Andrea said. "I was hoping that since Jill got her to come, maybe she'd have stayed for Sunday school, too. Oh, well."

"That would've been nice," Forrest said. He motioned past Andrea. "Here's another friend of ours! Maybe she'd like to stay for our class."

Andrea turned as Tracey and John approached.

"Hi, Coach," Tracey said. "Have you ever met John?" She introduced them to each other, then grabbed Andrea by the arm. "John has to head over to the rodeo arena for a meeting, and I thought I might stay for your class. That is, if the teacher will let me in."

"He will," Forrest said, "but be prepared. I run my Sunday school classes just as tough as I do my practices."

"Oh, wow, maybe I'd better go along with John after all," Tracey said seriously. "All they're going to do is practice riding bulls and easy stuff like that."

"You'll pay for that one in practice," the coach said with a laugh. "Come on. If we don't get into class, it'll be over before we can get started."

On Monday, Andrea was dying to ask Jill what Courtney thought of the church. She was also afraid to get the answer. Three times during the day she started to bring it up, and each time she stopped short of asking. By practice time, however, Courtney solved the problem.

"Your church was OK, Andrea," she said abruptly as they dressed in their practice gear. "At any rate, it's nicer than the ones I've been to on the military bases."

"Well, I'm glad you liked it," Andrea said slowly. "Sorry I didn't get to talk to you there. I was going to ask if you'd stay for Sunday school."

"Yeah, well, maybe sometime. I don't wanna O.D. on religion the first time out, you know." She laughed and Jill joined in. They left laughing, and Andrea wasn't entirely sure what kind of laugh it was.

Practice was ragged again that night, but on Tuesday the team hosted Spearfish and played a great game, defeating the Spartans by fifteen points. Jill did not start the game, but after coming in late in the second quarter and playing very well, Forrest started her in the second half and let her play most of the way. She seemed to have earned her way back into the coach's good graces by the game's end.

In the locker room, though, talk about the victory—which gave them a 9-3 record overall—was limited. Instead, conversation focused on the next night's planned Halloween party at Patty's.

"With no school Thursday, it won't matter about staying up late," Patty told them. "My mom says we can let it go until midnight if we want, as long as we don't get too noisy for the neighbors."

"They should be happy we're having the party," Betsy yelled. "It'll be the first excitement for them in years!"

"I thought no one here knew my neighbors," Patty said sarcastically.

"Well, we'll be quiet as lambs, that's for sure," Lara interjected. "I mean, everyone knows you can talk quietly, too, you know."

"Ooohh, which boy you planning to be talking quietly with?" Betsy asked.

"How many people you having?" Andrea chipped in when the laughter died.

"Mom says we can't have any more than thirty." She gave Andrea a little wink. "Don't worry, though, I made sure Matt is on the list."

That brought another big laugh, and Andrea turned red.

Andrea glanced over at Tracey. "You and John will be there, won't you?"

"Uh, I guess not," Tracey looked at Patty, and Patty looked away.

"What? Why not?"

Patty twisted around, an apologetic expression on her face, and spoke softly so only Andrea and Tracey could hear. The noise in the background was picking up again anyway, because Betsy had snuck up behind Jill and dumped baby powder on her head.

"I'm sorry, but my mom said only eighth graders," Patty said. "I tried to get her to change that." She looked quickly from Andrea to Tracey and back to Andrea again, an anguished look in her eyes. "Honest! I really did! I didn't like you so much earlier, Tracey, but I'm not against you anymore. I hope you believe that."

"Sure," Tracey said. "Hey," she coughed slightly, "I've gotta get going. See you tomorrow." She picked up her gym bag and left. Andrea grabbed her own bag and ran out of the locker room after her.

"Tracey, wait!"

Tracey stopped but didn't turn around.

"If you're not going to Patty's party, then I'm not either," Andrea said. "It's dumb that her mom won't let you come without John. She ought to make an exception."

"Don't be stupid," Tracey said angrily. "Don't cheat yourself out of a fun time because of me." Her angry eyes softened and she laid her hand on Andrea's shoulder. "Besides, John and I have another party to go to anyway. And if you don't go to Patty's, Matt's gonna be just miserable." She shook Andrea slightly to emphasize her point.

Three times that night Andrea woke up and vowed not to

go to the party. But after the last time, she dreamed of Matt and holding hands with him at the party's end.

She awoke confused and rumpled. *But why does it always seem like I'm being torn between my friends, God?* she asked.

"Should be fun tonight," Matt said as a large group sat eating in the cafeteria.

"You talking about that silly party of Patty's?" Courtney scoffed. "There's got to be more fun than that. Hey, it's Halloween!"

"So? What's wrong with a Halloween party on Halloween?"

"Oh, come on, there has to be bigger and better action than that," she answered, brushing back a lock of hair which had fallen over her right eye. "Don't you guys *ever* try anything exciting around here?"

"Oh, Courtney, shut up about this action garbage," Michelle said. "This isn't New York City or Chicago or someplace like that, you know. Just quit acting like a big shot, and come over to Patty's with the rest of us."

Courtney slammed her spoon down onto her tray and stood up. "You can do that baby stuff if you want, but I've got better things to do." She walked away and Jill stood up, glanced around the table, and trailed after her.

"There they go, the Action Girl and her faithful dog, Jill," Betsy smirked, drawing a laugh from the group.

"Better watch it, or Jill will stick a fist down your throat," one of the guys said. "I know I sure wouldn't want to tangle with her."

"Oh, I was just teasing," Betsy said. "I just wish Courtney would start realizing she's in a small town now. I get sick of her high-and-mighty attitude."

"After they check out all the other *action* tonight, they'll come to Patty's. You wait and see," Lara said.

"I hope so," Andrea said as the bell rang and everyone stood up. "It'd be just like them to do something dumb and get into trouble."

Coach Forrest's announcement met with groans. A curfew. How could he put on a curfew?

"But we don't even have school tomorrow," Patty moaned.

"I don't care. Tomorrow night's a big, big game for us, and if you stay up half the night and then sleep in late in the morning, you're going to play like you're half dead. Whether you like it or not, I want you home by 10:30—Halloween party or no Halloween party."

"But, Coach," the chorus of voices followed, almost in unison.

"Girls, we've been working all year for this. Do you want to play in the tournament or don't you?"

"Sure, but—"

"Then there's no buts about it. If we beat Deadwood tomorrow night, we're in. We're 9-3 overall and 8-2 in the conference. Hot Springs, Custer, Belle Fourche, and Deadwood are the only other contenders. If we beat Deadwood, they're out and we're in. It's as simple as that.

"Belle Fourche is going to get in for sure, so that leaves three spots for the other four teams," he continued. "If we lose at Deadwood, then we *have* to beat Rapid City North and hope Hot Springs can beat Custer at Custer. Now, what do you suppose those chances are?"

He stopped and was met with silence from the team.

"That's what I figured, too."

He picked up a basketball and slapped it between his palms.

"The curfew is on, and I'll be checking on you. If you're not in by 10:30, you sit out tomorrow night's game—no exceptions. Understood?" Again, he was met with silence, but slowly, one by one, the girls nodded in agreement. "You'll hate me tonight," he added, "but you'll thank me when we get into that tournament two weeks from now."

Practice sent downhill from there, and after forty-five minutes, Forrest tossed a basketball high into the air and blew his whistle.

"Go home!" he yelled. "And remember to have a good time at the party. The end of the world doesn't happen until 10:30!"

That brought a chuckle from Patty, and by the time they were in the locker room, everyone was talking and laughing again and remaking plans on how to pack the most into the party time available. By the time they left the gym, they had used up the remainder of the practice time just putting together more plans.

Andrea scarcely heard the youth group discussion. She noticed Matt was fidgeting, too. So was Jill. *But at least she's here!* thought Andrea with relief.

At last the time for the party came. By 7:30, nearly everyone had arrived at Patty's, and their first party of the year was under way.

Music blared out across the back lawn, and paper lanterns ringed the patio where they gathered. Patty was running around giving everyone balloons to blow up and tie to their ankles for a balloon-stomp game. Then she blew a whistle, and everyone chased each other, shrieking and trying to stomp other people's balloons.

It was after her balloon had been popped that Andrea noticed something disturbing.

"You know, it's almost 8:30 and Jill isn't here yet," she said to Matt, who was bending over and untying the bedraggled shred of his balloon from his ankle. "And neither is Courtney."

"Well, they're probably out checking the *action*," Matt winked. "You know, like Courtney said."

"Maybe." Andrea wrinkled her brow. "But Jill left the church when we did, didn't she?"

Matt nodded.

The game ended, and Andrea grabbed Matt's hand and pulled him over to where Patty was standing.

"You did invite Jill and Courtney, didn't you?"

"Sure," Patty responded. "I invited everyone on the team. I don't know why they aren't here."

"If they don't show up pretty soon, I might go call Jill's mom."

"Don't do that," Patty said. "They'll show up soon. You'll just get Jill in trouble with her mom and dad if you call."

"You're right, but I'm still worried." She walked over to the corner of the house and looked toward the front yard.

"Come on back to the party," Matt said. "Give them a little more time."

Andrea started back, heard the sound of a car approaching, and hurried around the corner of the house. Car lights swung onto the front yard, and the car stopped.

"Good! I'll bet they're here. Come on, Matt." She ran toward the car as Matt came up behind her. A figure emerged from the passenger side and took a couple of steps toward her.

"Hey, Jill, is that you?" Andrea shouted as she ran onto the front yard toward the car.

"Andrea?"

It was Tracey's voice.

"Tracey. What are you—I mean, hi. I thought you weren't coming."

"I'm not. John and I came here to look for you." Andrea walked up to Tracey and could see a worried look on her face. "Oh, hi, Matt," Tracey added as Matt joined them.

"How come you're looking for me?"

John leaned across the seat and looked out the window. "Because we need your help," he said. "Jill and Courtney are going to get themselves in some serious trouble if we don't stop them."

"Why? What's wrong?"

"I just came over from the garage, and some of the guys there said they heard how this bunch of sophomores and juniors were getting together to trash the principal's house and car tonight. And then Evan Postma said he heard there were a couple of eighth-grade girls going along, too. He told me who they were."

"Oh, man, we've got to stop them," Andrea said. "Where are they?"

"We don't know," Tracey answered. "But that's not the worst part."

"Yeah," John added. "The worst part is that Ev was yukking it up about how one of the guys got mad because he'd been taking out Courtney, and now she was going to be going with another guy tonight."

"There's not going to be a fight or anything, is there?" Matt asked.

"No. Probably worse. The guy went and told the police, and if any kids try anything at the principal's place tonight, the cops are going to be there waiting for them."

13
Suspension

"I can't say for sure, but it looks like there might be a few cars stopped up there by the old Willow Creek Bridge," John said, peering intently ahead as he turned the car north on a gravel road. "If that isn't them, I don't know where else to look. We've tried about everyplace else."

The trio had been driving around and through Sturgis for nearly forty minutes, and each place they hoped to find the group Courtney and Jill were with had turned up empty.

As they drew closer to the bridge, they could see half a dozen cars and a large group of kids.

"This has to be it." John pulled to a stop and opened the door. "Come on. Let's go see."

Andrea felt her stomach flip-flop as she climbed out. She was miles from where she was supposed to be, and only Matt knew why she had left the party. And she had sworn him to secrecy as she left.

The kids had a small fire going off to one side of the bridge, and in the flickering light, she caught sight of Courtney.

"Well, Courtney's here. I can see her."

"There's Jill, too," Tracey said at her shoulder. "Those dummies. What are they trying to prove?"

Tracey walked around Andrea and up to where the fire was burning. John joined her and immediately attracted a chorus of greetings from the group.

"We heard what you guys were thinking about doing and we came to get these two eighth graders out of here," John said. The others grew quiet as he spoke, then one of the boys stepped toward him.

"Maybe they don't want to leave," he said. "Maybe they'd like to be in on the fun, too."

"You call getting yourself arrested fun?"

"Who's getting arrested?" he hooted. "You're just trying to scare them into leaving our party."

"Yeah," Jill said, stepping forward. "We want to stay, so go away and leave us alone."

"Jill, you and Courtney are crazy," Andrea said. "Come on, get out of here now while you have a chance. John's not kidding. The police are going to end up getting you if you go along on this thing."

"Andrea? What are you doing out here?" Jill seemed shocked to hear her friend's voice.

"She came with us to get you because she cares about you," Tracey said. "And we care about you, too, Courtney. Please, both of you, get in the car with us and come back to town."

"Why should we?" Courtney said defiantly. "Give us one good reason."

"Because we don't want you to get in trouble." Tracey's voice was firm. "Maybe you don't think anyone cares about that, but I do, and Andrea does. Sure, you and I haven't been friends, but that doesn't mean I want you to get into trouble. And you may not know it, but there are other kids who care about you, too."

"You lie!" Courtney started to turn away as she spoke.

"Courtney, stop acting like an idiot!" Tracey cried. "You don't have to play hotshot with me. And you don't have to act like it's you against the world. I came out here to find you Jill. And I'm not leaving until you come!"

"You want to try and make us?" Jill threatened, stepping toward Tracey and doubling her right hand into a fist.

"Yes! I'm not going to let you guys get yourselves arrested!" Tracey clenched her own fists and tears came into her eyes. Andrea stared at her with amazement, but said nothing. "Now, if you want to fight me, I'll fight! At least you won't be running off to do something more stupid!"

Andrea held her breath and watched while Courtney and Jill exchanged glances. Her throat and lungs felt so tense they hurt. Behind her, she could feel John's nervousness, too, and hear him anxiously clench and unclench his own fists.

Finally, Jill spoke. "Okay," she said slowly. "I'll go with you." Andrea let out a small sigh of relief, and John took a step forward. Courtney stood watching as Jill walked toward Tracey, then shook her head.

"I didn't come out here to fight," she said with a half laugh. "Guess I'd better go, too. Better 'n causing some big scene, you know." She looked around, but everyone was standing uneasily, staring at Tracey.

John waited until all four girls were in the car, then backed over to it, got in, and wheeled the car around. He let out a long, slow sigh as he pulled away. "Courtney, you'll have to tell me where you live."

"She's staying over at my place," Jill said briefly. "Her dad's on duty tonight."

John drove back into town. No one spoke until he stopped in front of Jill's house, and she and Courtney started to get out. Jill paused, half in and half out.

"Would you really have fought us?" she asked.

"Yes," Tracey answered. "If it would've kept you from going with those kids."

"How come?"

"I don't know. I just didn't want you getting in trouble, that's all."

Jill shook her head. "You're weird, you know that? Half the time we can't even talk to each other, and the next thing you're out trying to *save* me." She shook her head again, jumped out, and slammed the door. John waited until he saw the girls go into the house, then headed for Andrea's.

"I don't care what Jill just said," Andrea said as they pulled up to her driveway. "I think you just kept them out of a lot of trouble, and I think she knows it. I'm glad you were there. Thanks." She smiled, and Tracey returned it.

"You better get inside. It's almost eleven o'clock."

Andrea gave a little yelp and jumped out, just in time to find herself bathed in the headlights of an oncoming car. The car pulled closer and slid to a stop, and all three of them looked over toward the driver. Andrea's eyes met Tracey's, and they both groaned.

It was Coach Forrest.

"You mean, Forrest caught you past curfew—personally?" Paula spoke with disbelief in her voice. They were standing in front of the drugstore.

"Yes. But we were just sitting by my driveway," Andrea replied. "It was dumb. We should've been inside."

"Especially Tracey," Paula answered. "It's a good half hour from your place to hers. How come you were still there, anyway? And how come you left the party like that? We never did find out where you went."

"We just went," Andrea said. "It's a long story, okay?"

"Suit yourself." Paula shrugged. "See you at the gym at three. Or won't you be going along?"

"I don't know yet. Forrest never said anything except to be there when the bus left for Deadwood. Then he drove off." Andrea felt miserable, and talking to Paula wasn't helping matters any. "I'll see you then. I gotta get going."

She started up the street on her bicycle and pulled over as a car honked and drove past. It was Jill and Courtney with Jill's mother. Both girls waved and smiled.

"Look at them," she said aloud. "I'm in trouble and they're both free as a breeze."

She rode home furiously, trying to take out her frustration by using up some energy. As she approached her driveway, she slowed. John's car was sitting there, and Tracey and John were standing beside it.

"Half the town must know we missed curfew," she said as she rode up. "I don't even know what to tell people. I don't want to tell them about Courtney and Jill."

"That's only half our problem," Tracey answered. "Did you hear what happened to the kids we left out there?"

"Yeah, they got picked up when they tried to trash the principal's house," Andrea said. "I already heard about it."

"They told the police you and I and John were there, too."

Andrea's mouth dropped open in disbelief. "What? Nobody's going to believe that." She stared at Tracey. "They *can't* believe that."

"John got a call from the principal just before lunch. He said he wanted to know if John was involved, because a couple of the kids who were arrested said he had been with them earlier, and some eighth-grade girls, too."

Andrea turned to John. "What did you tell him?"

"I said I went out where they were having a party. I picked up a couple of eighth-grade girls, and I took them home," he said. "I didn't tell them who."

Andrea sighed. "Sure, but everyone will think it was Tracey and me, not Jill and Courtney. What do we do?"

"What can we do?" Tracey asked.

"Nothing, I guess," Andrea said, sulking. "I just wish everyone knew why we went out there in the first place. We go do Jill and Courtney a favor and end up in trouble ourselves. It just isn't fair!"

"Maybe they'll say something," Tracey said hopefully. "No sense in us trying to make them look bad to make us look good. That'd probably just make us look even worse."

Andrea slumped against the car, feeling miserable. "You think the coach will suspend us?"

"Sure. Unless Jill and Courtney say something. Even then we'd probably get suspended, but they would, too. I'm almost hoping they don't say anything. No sense in all four of us getting kicked off the team."

"I wonder if your coach would listen if I explained that you two were trying to help Jill and Courtney," mused John.

"No! Don't!" Andrea said quickly. "Please?"

"Okay, okay," he said, holding up both hands. "I'll stay out of it, but I'll bet Jill and Courtney let you two take the rap. You wait and see."

At three, he dropped them at the gym, and when they entered the locker room, the other girls grew quiet. Then there was a knock on the door and Lara went to open it. She held it wide and Coach Forrest walked in.

He cleared his throat and motioned for them to sit down.

"Yesterday," he began, "I said that I wanted everyone home by 10:30. I said there would be no exceptions, and then I asked if everyone understood that rule." He paused. "Everyone told me that they did.

116

"Last night, I found two of our team members still out at eleven. I'm sure by now you all know all about it."

Andrea looked toward Jill, then Courtney, and then stared at the floor.

"We need this win tonight at Deadwood. But when I took this job, I also took on some responsibility to teach you to live by the rules. That's the way life is, like it or not. So, I'm going to have to suspend Andrea and Tracey for tonight's game."

The room was dead silent.

Lara shifted her feet and stood up.

"I, uh, I know about the rules, Coach, but the other girls and I were talking about this and we'd like to ask you to give them another chance."

"Thanks," Tracey said, standing as she spoke. "But the coach is right. We had a reason for missing the curfew, but we broke the rules. We're sorry for that. You'll just have to go to Deadwood and win without us."

"I want you along, too," Forrest added. "You can't play, but you can cheer for your teammates. Now, everyone on the bus. We'll be leaving in five minutes." He left the room, and Andrea angrily wiped a tear from her eye.

Both Jill and Courtney gathered up their game gear and left, but neither spoke to either Andrea or Tracey. The rest of the team filed past them one by one, and everyone gave them a reassuring pat on the shoulder as they passed.

The bus ride to Deadwood was the quietest all season. At the Deadwood gym, the girls dressed silently and came onto the court looking half beat already. Andrea and Tracey sat silently on the bench watching the warm-ups.

"If they keep acting like this, we're going to get creamed," Andrea said disgustedly. She walked onto the floor.

"You guys look sick out here," she said. "Tracey and I are the ones who blew it, but that doesn't mean the whole team has to lie down and die, does it? Come on! We've been saying all year how we're a team! Let's get fired up!"

She started clapping, and Tracey jumped up and ran over to join her. Paula grinned and grabbed a basketball, then dribbled in close and launched a hook shot that swept through the net.

"All right, Paula!" Betsy laughed. "Sky hook! We're gonna kill 'em."

The team was on fire by the opening tip and jumped out to an early lead as Paula scored on a hook, a driving lay-up, and a short jump shot. But Deadwood was a good team, too, and by halftime, the Scoopers had a one-point lead and three girls in foul trouble, including Courtney.

Courtney gulped a mouthful of water near the bench just before the second half was to begin; then she looked up at Andrea and Tracey.

"I'm sorry," she mumbled. "We really need you two out there, and *you* shouldn't be sitting there."

"Well, just play tough!" Andrea cut her off, and Courtney stiffened. "We can still win this game if you do!" Then Andrea's voice softened. "Hey," she said. "Don't worry about the other."

"Thanks," Courtney said. She reached out both hands and grabbed Andrea's left hand and Tracey's right. "Thanks. I'll try my best."

Deadwood controlled the second-half tip, but Courtney cut in front of the girl with the ball, stole the pass, and dribbled in to score. Andrea and Tracey gave her a thumbs-up signal as she passed, and she returned the gesture. From that point, she played better and better on offense, scoring three more baskets and stealing the ball another time. But early in the fourth quarter, she stumbled as she tried to get another steal and fell into the Deadwood girl with the ball.

The referee blew his whistle and Courtney had her fifth foul. She walked slowly over to the bench, sat down, and buried her head in her arms. Andrea and Tracey each gave her a pat on the shoulders.

A minute later, Paula drew her fifth foul, and the Scooper players looked panic stricken. Deadwood quickly capitalized, working the ball inside time and again to score against the weakened Sturgis front line.

With less than a minute remaining, Deadwood took the lead for the first time, then hung on to win. After shaking hands with their opponents, the Scoopers walked dejectedly into their locker room with Forrest trailing. Before he could say anything, Courtney stepped in front of him and waved her arms. Her eyes were streaked where her tears and mascara had mixed, but her mouth was set firmly.

Everyone stopped.

"I let you down tonight," she began, "because I shouldn't have been on the floor. I should have been on the bench, and Andrea and Tracey should have been out there."

Andrea swallowed hard and looked over at Tracey. She was staring at Courtney.

"The reason they were late last night, Coach, was because of me. I was out with that bunch who was going over to the principal's place, and they came out and got me. They kept me from getting into trouble, and because of that *they* got into trouble." She almost started to cry again, but turned her head away until she got control of herself again. "It's—the first time anyone ever cared enough to do anything like that for me, and—I didn't know what to do." She snuffled loudly. "I—should have told you before the game, but, well . . . ."

She wiped her face with her sleeve, and Coach Forrest went over and put his arm around her shoulders and gave her a big squeeze.

Jill stood and turned toward the team, clearing her throat slightly.

"It wasn't just Courtney," she said softly. "I was out there last night, too. If Andrea and Tracey hadn't come, we might have been arrested. I should have said something, but I was afraid what my mom and dad might do if they found out." She hung her head. "I'm sorry."

She walked over to where Tracey was standing and held out her hand.

"Thanks for last night, and for taking all the heat today. Okay?"

Tracey smiled and grabbed Jill's hand, and then gave her a big hug.

Suddenly, the whole team was crowded around them, hugging Andrea and Tracey and Jill and Courtney, too. Everyone was laughing and talking at the same time.

"Hey, Scoopers!" Forrest interrupted them with a shout. "Are we a team, or what?"

They all cheered in response.

"Okay," he smiled. "Let's go home."

14
Sky Hook Again

"We can still make the tournament if we win, right?"

Andrea's question was directed to the coach as they wrapped up their final practice before the Rapid City North game. It was the final game of the regular season.

"Yes, *if*," he said. "And that's a big if. If Hot Springs beats Custer at Custer and we win, we'll be tied with Hot Springs and Custer for the third best record. But because we beat Custer, we'll be picked ahead of them. Belle Fourche and Deadwood are in for sure.

"All *we* have to do is beat North, and they're 13-0."

"Aw, Coach, it'll be a snap," Betsy said. "I don't know what you're worried about. Just because they're all six footers doesn't mean they're better than us." Everyone laughed, and Forrest grimaced.

"I'm just hoping you can see the basket through all those trees. Besides being tall, they also wear green uniforms, you know."

"I can see the headlines now," Patty said, stretching out her fingers as if reading along a newspaper headline. " 'Scoopers Chop Down Forest!' " she stopped, looked at Coach Forrest, and giggled. "Uh, I mean 'Trees.' "

"Funny, Patty. Really funny," he said dryly. Then he started to chuckle, too. "You know, it is kind of funny, though. I've got an even better headline."

He paused and looked up as if reading: " 'Forrest Leads Scoopers Past Trees.' Kind of gets you right here, doesn't it?" he said clutching at his heart.

"That's for sure," Betsy said as everyone groaned. "Heartburn!"

"Get out of here," he shouted good-naturedly, and they scrambled off the court.

Andrea had another bad case of butterflies as she finished lacing up her shoes in the visitors' locker room at North Junior High.

"I feel almost like it's opening game, or something," she half whispered to Tracey as Tracey walked over and stood peering into the mirror while she tied back her hair. "How you doin'?"

"Okay." Tracy dropped her brush and watched it clatter across the floor. "Uh, maybe a little nervous," she laughed. "What's with us tonight, anyway? You'd think we hadn't played all year."

She went to retrieve the brush, while Andrea stood and checked her hair and looked carefully at herself in the mirror. "I feel like I've changed a lot," she said as Tracey returned. "It seems like so long ago that we went out for that first practice, and now it's almost over. Feels weird."

"You have changed," Tracey said. "We all have. Being on this team has helped everyone grow up. I'm glad I decided to try. Thanks."

She reached over and patted Andrea's shoulder. Andrea smiled in return. "Come on, don't start getting all gushy. We've got a tough game ahead, and we need to get ready."

"Yeah, we need to get mean!" Tracey made a face at the mirror. "How's this?"

Andrea laughed. "It won't scare 'em, but they might get weak from laughter. Go try it on Jill. If she laughs we've got 'em."

Tracey gave her a shove and then screamed and ducked as Andrea turned on the faucet and grabbed a handful of water to throw at her.

They were interrupted by a pounding on the door, and Andrea tossed the water into the sink and rubbed her hands on the sides of her uniform jersey as Paula ran to open it. It was Forrest.

"Hi, Coach," she said brightly, clasping her hands behind her back and trying not to laugh.

"I'm not even going to ask," he said with a sigh. He motioned toward the benches in front of him, and the girls all came and sat down.

"Well, this is it. I'm not going to make any long speeches. I think you're as ready to play as you can be, and I know you'll go out and do your best. They want us to come out and stay on the floor until halftime, so we'll say our team prayer now, and then go out and get warmed up."

The girls stood and gathered in a circle.

"Everybody ready?" Forrest asked. "If so, I'll—"

"Coach?"

The team members, many of whom had started to bow their heads, looked up in surprise as Courtney spoke.

"Uh, Coach, if it's okay—with you and—and the team, I've got something I'd like to say."

There was a long pause. *What now?* Andrea caught herself thinking, then felt ashamed. Courtney had come so far this year. Coach Forrest broke the silence.

"Courtney, I can't speak for the team, but I know I'm always ready to listen to what you have to say." Heads nodded here and there.

"Thanks," she said thickly. "But, ah, first—I'd like—to be part of this circle." And she stepped forward. Andrea's eyes widened, and a little murmur ran around the group. Paula reached over and took Courtney's right hand, and Jill grabbed her left. One by one, the rest of the girls and the coach joined hands.

Courtney cleared her throat. "Well, I just want to say, uh, that sometimes some of us kids can be pretty dumb. Sometimes we don't know it when we're blessed with friends—really good friends." She looked quickly around the circle, ducked her head, then lifted it almost defiantly and continued.

"And I want you to know I'm proud to be a part of this team!" She lowered her head and Andrea thought she saw a tear splash on the floor. She felt a lump coming to her own

122

throat as she heard Courtney's next words. "And I'm real sorry for having hurt some of you this year. I didn't mean it."

Several other girls were looking teary eyed as Courtney raised her head and smiled broadly. "I know you're all going to do great out there tonight," she said. "But, you know, it doesn't matter if we win or lose. You're all winners to me!"

"All right!" boomed Coach Forrest. "Let's pray. Lord, I'd just like to add my *Amen* to what Courtney has said. Amen"

Andrea blinked, and then she realized he was right spite of herself, Courtney really had been talking to God, well as to them. *God, you are amazing,* thought Andrea. *Ta. about changing someone!*

Then they were all crowding around Courtney again, crying together and hugging her. Coach Forrest, too, was wiping tears from his eyes. He hugged Courtney, too, and backed away and picked up a towel to wipe off his face.

"Anyone need a crying towel?" he said, holding it up. "It's slightly used." He laughed and the girls started passing the towel around.

"Even if we do lose," Andrea said loudly, "what just happened made the season a success as far as I'm concerned." The others echoed her response, and Courtney glowed.

Forrest held up both hands and asked for quiet.

"Girls, I'm proud of you and what you've accomplished this season. Now, let's go out and play some basketball."

They crowded together, clasped hands and screamed, "Let's go, Scoopers!" then spilled out onto the gym floor with barely enough time to warm up before the opening game buzzer sounded.

As Forrest had predicted, the North team was good. And they were big. But the Scoopers were fired up and ready to play. The game seesawed back and forth throughout the first half. The North team players not only were big, but they were rough.

Midway through the second quarter, one of the big, quick North guards charged past Lara, made a nifty move around Paula, and ran head-on into Andrea. Andrea went down hard and for a few seconds saw stars. When she could focus again, it was Coach Forrest's anxious face she saw first.

"You okay?"

"Sure." She tried to stand, and sat back down. "I think."
Paula and Tracey knelt beside her and she smiled. "I think I
got hit by a tree," she said. Paula's worried look changed to a
grin.

"You leaving her in, Coach, or taking her out?" the referee
inquired.

"Out," the coach answered. "I think her brain got
scrambled," he laughed. The referee gave him an odd look
and shrugged, and Forrest motioned for Michelle to check in.

With two minutes left in the second quarter, it was Jill's
turn to go down, but this time it was not a laughing matter.
As she took a pass from Patty and turned to drive to the
basket, Jill suddenly registered a look of shock, then fell in
agony.

Andrea was the first one to her side.

"My ankle," Jill gasped. "I felt something snap. It feels
like it's on fire." She moaned and lay back, holding both
hands over her eyes. Forrest sprinted over from the bench,
checked the ankle, and called for an ice bag. Arnell hurried
over with a bag from the Sturgis bench, and the North coach
brought one over, too.

Together, the coaches carried Jill to the sidelines and
wrapped an ice bag on either side of the injured ankle.

"I think it's just a sprain," Forrest said. "You sit up here
behind our bench and keep that foot elevated."

The game was under way again, and the half ended with
Sturgis trailing by four. With Jill out, the North guards
were taking the ball right past Lara and Patty, and neither
seemed to have the courage to try to stop them as Jill had.

"We'll stay out here and talk," Forrest said as the team
gathered around the bench where Jill was sitting. "Lara, I'm
putting Arnie in for you. We'll try to do something about
those big guards of theirs. Forwards and centers, keep
playing tight inside, and don't let their big girls get to the
ball. If we keep them outside and do something about their
guards, we've got a chance.

"Their big girls are big, but they aren't very good shooters
from anywhere outside of eight to ten feet. Okay?

"Andrea, Courtney, and Paula, you've got to start
shooting more. If you don't put up the shots, we won't have a

chance. Now, let's get back on the court and work on your favorite shots." They started to move away. "And then take them in the second half!" he called after them over the crowd noise.

The second half got under way with a bang—a bad bang for Sturgis. The six-foot-one North center tipped the ball out long to a forward, who fed a pass to one of the guards, who connected from fifteen feet with Patty nearly hanging on her.

"Lucky!" Andrea said to Patty as she ran past shaking her head in disbelief. "You were playing her tough. Keep it up."

Andrea set up near the free throw line, then cut to the corner as Arnie lobbed the ball in to Paula. Paula took two dribbles toward the middle and turned and bounced a pass back to Andrea, as Andrea's defensive player reacted to Paula's move.

Andrea put up the shot and watched it fall through.

The next time down the court, though, the big North forward stayed in position, and one of the big guards sagged back to help. No shot at all, Andrea thought. She looked back to the guard spot and saw Patty in the open. Andrea pivoted away from the defense and lobbed the ball to Patty.

Patty's shot went wide.

North scored again, and Sturgis retaliated on a foul and two free throws by Paula; but when Sturgis once more had the chance to close the gap, a guard shot—this time by Arnell—went wide. North tried to hurry the ball upcourt on the exchange and threw it away, and Patty turned and called for a time-out.

Forrest jumped up to meet the team as they came off the floor.

"What's up? Why the time-out?"

"Coach, you gotta take me out and move Tracey out there," Patty panted as she spoke. Tracey gave her a surprised look.

"Why?"

"Because neither Arnie or I can get a decent shot, and those guards of theirs know we can't shoot. They're just backing in there to help stop our inside players. We need somebody out there who can shoot." She reached over and grabbed Tracey by the arm. "Her."

"Okay," the coach said. "We're still four down and less than eight minutes left in the game. Go ahead, Tracey. Check back in. And from here on out, I want the guards to go into a full-court press. Stay on the ball all the time. Paula. You play right about mid-court, and the two forwards stay back." They clasped hands as the buzzer sounded. "Let's win for Jill!" he said loudly as the crowd noise intensified. They looked toward Jill.

"For Jill!" they shouted, breaking the huddle.

Sturgis patiently passed the ball around the perimeter as North went into a zone defense, and as the third quarter drew to a close, Paula made a move toward the basket. As the defense collapsed around her, she passed back to Tracey, who put up an arcing shot from just outside the free throw line. The ball ripped through the net at the buzzer, and Sturgis was back within two.

"Keep being patient on offense, and remember to press on defense," Forrest said. "We're going to surprise them, and we have to make our shots count."

The North center controlled the final tip, but the ball was slapped away by Arnell, who kept her dribble and waited for her teammates to set up. For nearly three minutes, the Scoopers passed and waited, then a North guard overplayed the ball, and Tracey quickly took the open shot and scored. Now they were tied, and the home fans began urging their team on.

The North girls started the ball upcourt and froze as Arnell and Tracey suddenly came charging upcourt to put on defensive pressure. The guard on Arnie's side flipped the ball toward her teammate, who wasn't prepared for the pass. Tracey dived for the ball, grabbed it, and tossed a pass toward Arnie while laying on her back.

Arnie went in uncontested for the lay-up and Sturgis had the lead for the first time. North called time.

"All right, all right!" Forrest greeted them, clapping his hands. "Now, remember, be patient and play sticky defense. Even if they score, we'll still be tied and have the ball. Don't take a bad shot!"

The girls passed the water bottle around, and Paula went from girl to girl with words of encouragement. The buzzer

126

sounded, and they broke the huddle. The crowd noise was becoming deafening.

Tracey and Arnie hounded the ball handlers all the way up the court, then fell back into the tight Sturgis zone, forcing North to keep the ball outside. The crowd grew louder. Andrea wiped the back of her hand across her forehead as perspiration began getting into her eyes. She peered at the clock. Less than a minute.

The ball came to her side, and the forward looked ready to shoot. She yelled and jumped toward her, and the girl bounced the ball past and in to the big center. Paula held her ground and held her hands high, but the girl got away the shot anyway.

Everyone froze for a couple of seconds as the ball bounced around the rim, then, almost in slow motion, it started to fall away. Andrea could hear Forrest screaming above the crowd, yelling for them to block out and get the ball.

The ball came off their side, and Andrea stepped in front of her girl to keep her away. Paula leaped high and tipped the ball, and it just eluded the outstretched fingers of the North center and came straight for Andrea's face. Almost in self-defense, she pulled up her hands and grabbed.

The center and the forward turned together to try to get the ball back, and Andrea turned between them and saw Tracey out of the corner of her eye. She thrust the ball toward her in desperation, then fell. When she looked up, Tracey was dribbling full speed toward the other basket.

"Go for it!" she screamed. Both North guards were running with her step for step, and the clock was ticking down. Suddenly, Tracey pulled up, glanced toward the clock and looked back for help. Seeing none, she turned sideways and put up a "sky hook."

From the floor, Andrea watched as the ball looped through the air, hit the back of the rim, bounced high, and fell through as the final buzzer sounded. She leaped to her feet, screaming, and the Sturgis players surrounded Tracey, laughing and cheering wildly.

The crowd had grown silent. Slowly, some of the fans began to applaud; then everyone broke into a round of applause for the Sturgis girls.

They were still celebrating twenty minutes later after dunking each other in the shower and getting changed and ready for the bus ride home. Forrest had helped Jill on board and was sitting talking with her as the rest of the team joined them.

"Are we in the tournament?" Betsy asked before anyone had even gotten settled.

Forrest shook his head. "No. I don't think so. I called down to Custer, and the game had four minutes left, and Custer was leading by eight points. Looks like they'll be in, and we'll be watching."

Everyone grew quiet. Betsy stood again.

"Well, we may be out, but we showed everyone tonight that we'll be ready for next year. Watch out for the Scoopers!" she yelled, and everyone joined her in a wild round of screaming and stomping.

The bus ride home was almost quiet as the girls sat talking softly among themselves about the season and the game. As they pulled into the school parking lot, Andrea saw her mother waving excitedly to her. She waved back.

The driver opened the door, and Andrea's mother hurried to get on.

"Congratulations, girls!" she yelled. "We heard about your great win! Now it's on to the tournament!"

"I'm afraid we didn't make it," Coach Forrest said. "Custer—"

"Lost!" she burst out. "Mrs. Bradford called her sister in Custer about ten minutes ago, and Hot Springs won that game. You girls are in the tournament!"

The coach sat back down in shock, and Andrea turned to Jill and hugged her happily. Behind them the rest of the team was shrieking and hugging and jumping up and down. Andrea beamed as she watched Courtney and Tracey hugging each other.

"Tracey!" she yelled. "Better keep practicing that sky hook!"

Then she glanced up and added, "Don't worry about yours, God. It's working just fine."